Nine Lives

A Paranormal Adventure
Bad Tom Series: Book Three

I0554045

Jill Nojack

IndieHeart Press
Kent, Ohio

Cover and interior designed by IndieHeart Press.

www.jillnojack.com

Publisher's Note: This is a work of fiction. Names, characters, places, and incidents are a product of the author's imagination. Any resemblance to actual people, living or dead, or to businesses, companies, events, or institutions, is completely coincidental.

Nine Lives / Jill Nojack. -- 1st ed.
ISBN: 978-0-9911234-8-3

DAY DRIFTS SLOWLY into Giles Woods. It takes time for the early autumn light to break through from gray to dappled shade. I listen to the night things putting themselves to bed while it turns. Cat wants the hunt, but I hold him back: I hold myself back. Today, I'll hunt the things of the light that shuffle around the forest's damp, mulched floor as the sun rises.

A skinny mutt comes snuffling toward me, drawn by the smell of the fresh kill I brought down and laid out as a lure. It has to be part whippet or greyhound with that scrawny body and jutting spine. I almost feel sorry for it. Almost. But dogs are filthy, smelly things. No self-respecting cat would befriend an unwashed stray.

I hunker down on Cat's strong haunches, getting ready to spring, surprise it, give chase, when a growl sounds from the brush on the other side of the small clearing.

A large black dog, thick in the middle with swollen teats, teeth bared, moves out from the undergrowth, and stands ready to fight. The half-starved mutt hunches down, fear in its eyes, then slinks back and away from the breakfast it won't have today, bony tail between its legs. It fades into the woods and is gone. It's only me and her now.

Finally. The other strays I've captured were only practice for today. Cat's tail twitches as the dog moves into the clearing, sniffing at the newly dead baby rabbit and then quickly gobbling it up, bones crunching as it eats. It's better fed than the dog it chased off, but scruffier than a week or two ago when Robert buried his son's ashes. Although she's less well fed, she's bigger around the middle. Nearly ready to drop those pups.

Cat responds to my adrenalin and tenses. This isn't just any dog.

We burst into the clearing and face off with our prey, back arched, lips pulled back to display our pointy fangs.

But it's a ploy. A charade. It's all part of the plan. The stupid thing goes for it: dogs are so dumb.

I turn with feline grace and launch away, my hindquarters staying out of range of the dog's snapping jaws. The demon can growl, it can snap, but it can't outrun sleek me in its underfed, pregnant shell.

I hear hard breathing and the whisk of branches whipping against its body as I dart through holes in the brush wide enough for a clever cat but calculated to give a dog plenty of trouble. My victims never catch the scent of the other unfortunates who followed me through this path. They never catch on until it's too late.

Grasping jaws brush against our tail when they bite down. Too close. I spur Cat on to move faster. We're nearly there now. Just one more break in the brush to run through and then...

Metal bars close around us. The dog is a whisker behind, twigs snapping as it follows us in.

Nowhere to go but up.

I leap through the open door at the top, then neatly slap it shut with one paw and wait for the dog to hit the end of the cage with a thud-clank before I pull the pin at the back with my mouth and the spring-loaded trap door goes slamming down.

The dog bites at the top of its prison uselessly as I stare down into its eyes. Cat can't see reds, no cat can, but I'm sure it's Anat. I'm sure the dog's eyes have the red glint of the demon inside.

Unlike most of the mutts I've captured, it doesn't bark or whine to be let out. It knows what I am.

I move to where I've left my clothes and think my shift words, *good Tom.* My warm black fur becomes pale skin as my bones pull themselves apart, morph, grow, stretch, and my human body appears where only moments before, the cat had been. Focused on my victory, I barely notice the pain.

I get dressed, then turn back to the dog in the cage. Its eyes have a red sheen, angry and defiant. I knew it. I knew it was her.

I usually get a rope around the dog's neck and leave it tied up by the road for the dogcatcher. Then I take off after dropping a call. But I'm not taking any chances with this one.

I open my pack and take out the customized witches' salt Natalie made me. I've been waiting a long time to use it: I have no magic of my own to make spells, but she assured me it will bind Anat to the dog's body as it dies, finally forcing her out of the world of the living where she hasn't belonged for a thousand years. I have to trust that Natalie knows what she's doing. It wasn't easy planning this without Cassie finding out that Anat might still be a threat. After what she went through, no one could bear to tell her.

I sprinkle the powder and say the words to activate the spell as I ready myself to open the cage and sink the knife in at her heart.

The dog's eyes never blink. They follow mine as I work. There's a slight sedative effect to the powder, and she sinks to the floor of the cage, her eyes losing their glow. They're just dog eyes now: brown, pleading, sad.

And, of course, the phone rings. Portable phones. Great idea. Hooray for progress.

I snatch it from my pocket. Robert.

I greet him with, "It's done. I got her. Anat."

He doesn't answer right away, then he says, "You're sure it's Anat and not Mrs. Green's Fluffy?"

"Yeah, yeah…I never laid a hand on Fluffy…."

"That better be the truth, Tom. Lavinia is frantic. Woke me up for the second morning in a row, insisting that there are evil forces in this town bent on coming between senior citizens and their pets. Says dogs are disappearing at an alarming rate in the past week or two."

"Sheesh. What does it look like?"

"She's a Yorkie mix. Wears a jeweled collar. Just about the last dog you'd mistake for an unloved stray."

Oh hell. "I'll keep an eye out for it."

"If you would. And I hope that your obsession with the town's strays is finally at an end?"

"I don't know why you call it an obsession. A few feral dogs…"

"If you say so, Tom." He pauses. I imagine him wearing his patient look. "Of course, I'm still hoping for Fluffy's safe return."

We say our goodbyes, and the dog looks up at me again with its I-can't-help-it-that-I'm-possessed eyes.

Cat's still pushing hard for the dog's demolition, but there's always plan B. I'd fight her to the death if I had to, but the dog isn't threatening me now. Reluctantly, I put the knife away.

I call animal control about an abandoned dog and drop a little extra intel about a Yorkie mix that might have come their way two days before and that might belong to a Mrs. Lavinia Green on Spruce street, if they wanted to ring her up and ask. Then I fade into the bushes to wait.

No one's going to adopt a pregnant dog before its kill day arrives in a week. Who would want a whole houseful of slobbering animals at one time?

The animal control officer arrives in the city's white van. He looks surprised by the cage, but he's a big guy. He has no problem loading it in and driving away.

I think about slipping back into the woods as Cat, but it's a beautiful day, crisp not cold. It smells like sunshine.

Nah, this is a good day to take that walk back into town as a man.

***

It's been eight days since I walked out of the woods as a man and sent Anat on her way to the pound. I was caged there once myself, thanks to Anat's buddy Kevin, so it's etched in my memory permanently that Thursday is kill day at the pound. If an animal is unlicensed and no one claims or adopts it, that's the end of it. And the pound has been full up for a while, thanks to my efforts. Maybe Robert is almost right about my watchfulness having slid into obsession. I don't think they'll be making any humane exceptions for a pregnant dog, but I need to be sure.

I dial animal control and trap my phone against my ear as I open the fridge and rummage for the makings of an amazing breakfast. Cassie won't know what we're celebrating, but that doesn't matter. Eggs Benedict, I think. The ingredients are lined up on the counter by the time someone answers.

"I'm calling about a lost dog?"

"Talk fast. We're euthanizing today."

"Black dog? Female?"

"Yeah, we've got one. Yours pregnant?"

"No. Can't be mine. She only went missing yesterday and wasn't pregnant then."

"That's a shame. Hate to put them down when they're in a family way. Wouldn't happen to want another one?"

"No. Sorry, can't help you out. So, the poor thing's done for today? Even though she's pregnant?" I try not to start dancing, but my feet are itching to do a celebration cha-cha.

"Yeah, she's scheduled. If you want to leave a number, I can get back to you if another black female comes in."

"And...man, do you believe it? That's her scratching at the back door. Sorry to bother you.

I've got a hole in the fence I've got to fix. You have a good one."

Cassie walks in on the last part, plants a kiss on me, and says, "We don't have a fence."

"I have no idea why that would pop in my head as an excuse to get rid of that salesman, but..."

She's not even listening anymore as she sticks her head around my shoulder to eye up what I'm cooking. "So, that looks pretty good," she says. Her lips smack close to my ear.

I set my utensils down, turn toward her, and draw her in close in silent appreciation of her appetites before I turn back to finish making our victory breakfast. In a few hours, we'll finally be free.

I unlock the front door to the Giles Gallery of Art and call out, "Dash?". But my elegant, elderly boss doesn't appear, smirk on his face, saying, "That boyfriend of yours finally let you get here on time, Cassie?"

It's strange for the gallery to be locked when I arrive, but I'm not going to worry just yet: I can tell Dash has been here. Above the smell of new white paint from last month's cleansing coat, it smells like clove and vanilla. Dash's passage always leaves a scented wake of mustache wax and herbal cigarettes.

So, maybe he went out. But it's really not like him to close up shop in the middle of the day. Still, if he was here, he'd have heard the chime when I came in. And he always floats to the front of the shop no matter what he's doing when the art-lover-signaling chime rings.

Go figure. On the day I finally show up early to make up for the fact that Tom's goodbye kisses almost always make me late, the boss isn't even here.

Not that I wanted to skip the kisses; that would be impossible. Ever since he stopped going out every morning as Cat, I've been late for work because nobody would skip kisses with Tom on purpose. But there was this cute little puppy scratching at the door of the shop this morning, and I had to play with it. It was the sweetest thing! I couldn't keep my eyes or my hands off of it.

Anyway, that made me pretty much smell like dog, which made Tom pretty much not want to be near me. It's a Cat thing, I guess. I washed, but he said he could still smell it. His nose is really sensitive.

With Tom not in a mood for smooches, I thought Dash could get out of here for an extra long lunch with Jon. He's such a great boss. He should have a chance to linger with his partner like he tolerates me lingering with mine. I'm kind of disappointed he's not here. I would have loved to surprise him.

So now, I don't know if he wants me to open the gallery or not. We'll miss the lunch crowd, or the lunch trickle, or whatever you want to call it, if I don't. Even a trickle can produce a buyer or two out of the flow. And we definitely treasure those buyers among the looky-loos.

Plus, now that Dash has the gallery back in his

name free and clear, he's super excited about it again. He's even extended the hours now that I can give him some time off once in a while. It really is weird that he's not here.

"Dash?" I call again, and I hear the sound of scuffling coming from the back room. Okay, so maybe he was caught up with something else and didn't hear me. I push aside the soft crimson curtain that separates the gallery from the employee room and storage areas.

Whoa! There's something I've never seen before. A trap door in the floor? The red-based oriental rug that normally covers it must have been doing its job. I would never have guessed there was anything under it.

Wait, Tom told me about it: there's a hidden storage room below the gallery. He said Dash helped hide Anat's magic boxes there when my friends were trying to figure out how to get her spirit out of my body.

Darn it. I don't want to think about that. But here it is again. Always lurking around, tainting my childhood memories with the knowledge that my Granny wasn't really my Granny. No, she'd been possessed by an ancient, evil, demon-goddess who was only interested in me because she wanted to harvest my body when Granny Eunice's gave out.

Seriously, as dysfunctional families go, mine ranks right up there.

And then I realize that maybe something bad

happened to Dash if he's not answering. I call down the stairwell, and he doesn't respond. I need to get down there. He's not a young guy. He could be in trouble.

The stairs are steep and the risers are narrow. Not much light, either. It sneaks through a slit created by an almost closed door at the bottom of the stairs.

I hold the handrail as I cautiously make my way step by step and call again, "Dash? Are you down here?"

The only answer is a long, low, rumbling growl.

I stop with one foot frozen in the air, unable to finish my next step forward. I stand there for a long moment, afraid to move. What the? My heart races as my mind reviews the possibilities. Gremlins? Zombies? Demons? Beliebers?

I get myself back under control, unfreeze my foot, and move it backward, my chest tight and buckets of adrenalin dumping into my system. I swear I can hear the blood coursing through my veins hard and fast.

I'll get out of here and go for Tom. He'll know what to do.

As my foot taps behind me, seeking the step, and my eyes are still fixed on the semi-darkness below, Dash's head and shoulders appear, peeking out around the half-closed door.

Omigod, what a relief! You'd have to know

Dash to understand, but he's probably the least scary thing in the entire town of Giles. He's gentle and pliable and is always the first person to wave the white flag when someone needs to surrender. Now I just want to laugh at myself, but I'm afraid he'd take it the wrong way, and I would never want to hurt his feelings. He's a total sweetie.

"Cass?" he says. "Oh my, you gave us quite a turn."

He looks disheveled—even his dyed-black mustache isn't pomaded up at the ends in homage to Salvador Dali like usual. It droops above his upper lip, a hairy, unkempt caterpillar.

Then Jon pops his head out above Dash's shoulder, smoothing down his normally perfectly-coiffed white hair. "Hello, Cass. You've come across us unawares, I'm afraid. Can we have a moment, do you think?"

Great. I've interrupted the boss's freak time. That growl? Wow. A little role play? I try not to think about it, but I don't have much success. Now I'm imagining the guys dressed up in a little something furry. Ew. Yuck. Ick on the senior sexy.

But wait a minute—I mean, really—who am I to get all judgey? My hot, werecat boyfriend gets furry on a regular basis.

I make my way up the stairs with a smirk on my

face. Good for them. I mean it. I hope Tom and I

are still as playful when we're that age.

***

I busy myself with the dusting while I wait for the guys to finish up whatever they're doing down there, making sure I get the backs of the frames the way Dash likes it done. I'd grab the step stool from the back room and really get into it, but I don't want to leave the gallery unattended. We've got some small brasses on display that would be way too easy to stick in a backpack or purse.

When he does appear, he looks a little out of it, still not quite himself. Not nervous like he usually is, just...I don't know. Absent? Jon follows him and has pretty much the same expression.

"So sorry," I say. "I didn't mean to interrupt anything."

Dash says, "Never go downstairs again unless I say so. There will be consequences." He's like Mr. Serious all of a sudden. And his eyes are tight with fury. So not Dash.

"Really, I'm sorry. I promise I won't do it again. I just...well, I got here early so you guys could have a longer lunch than usual. A special treat, you know?"

His tight expression loosens a little, and then Jon puts a hand on his shoulder and gives it a squeeze, and they're mostly back to normal. But just mostly. Dash gives me a smile but it looks forced.

"That's kind of you, Cass. Of course, we'd love to spend some extra time together. It may be one of the last warmish days to take a walk around town before the sun goes away for the winter."

He looks back at Jon, who adds, "True, and we wouldn't want to waste it."

They exit the shop, Jon's hand still on Dash's shoulder.

Thank goodness that storm didn't last long. And no way am I ever going near that hatch again. I don't care what's down there, I love this job. I'd rather deal with a zombie invasion than Dash's mustache-quivering anger!

Tom will get a laugh out of it, though. Me getting terrified in the art gallery, of all places, by my boss's sexy-time sound effects. I make a mental note to tell him the whole silly story when I get home.

I PROMISED CASSIE I'd have plenty of time to take inventory today to make up for not being able to pitch the woo this morning. Because she stank like dog. I mean, I haven't been out hunting them for two months, but that doesn't mean I want my girl to smell like one.

It's past the shop's best season now despite the warm day, so I won't be busy waiting on people. But I'm not sure now that I can keep my promise. I keep drifting off, thinking about other things. I'm cat-brained today, distracted by every little movement.

The multi-color potion bottles in the front window create interesting lights and shadows across the shop floor when people pass, interrupting the sunlight. I want to jump them, skitter across the floor as they appear and move, then disappear again.

I definitely haven't been letting Cat hunt enough. It's so hard to tear myself away from Cassie to give him his own time despite how much I owe my animal side.

Inventory is drudgery. I'd rather think about the eternally pompous pigeon outside the window that would make a great meal for my alter ego. And Cassie's smile—I love thinking about that. I could do it all day. Usually do. And, of course, there's the ring: I've pretty much put away every dime I've earned at the shop so that I can get a good one. That's because, when it really comes down to the nitty-gritty, there's only one thing in this big, wide world that I want, and that's Cassie by my side for the rest of my life, however long that might be.

My eyes are drawn to the pigeon again as it struts along the top of the bench. Not my fault: it moved. I had to track it.

Okay, so I only want two things. If I end up with everything I've ever hoped for, why shouldn't Cat's dreams come true, too? He's certainly earned a juicy pigeon dinner. But that's it. Those two things. It's not a long list. Just my ring on Cassie's finger and Cat's belly full of freshly-killed bird.

***

The shop bell rings, and I come out from around a shelf full of colorful potions in vintage glass to see Robert there, looking around expectantly. When he sees me, we head for each other and shake hands; man, I'm glad to see him. More ladies visit the shop then men over the course of the day, and there's only so much small talk a man can listen to before he needs some good ol' masculine back-slapping, highly communicative grunting, and companionable silence.

"Anything I can help you find, Robert?"

"Already found it. I came here looking for you."

"What's up?" I move off a little as I catch an unpleasant odor nearly covered by the smell of Old Spice. "Other than tracking in the smell of some hairy little beast?"

"What?" He looks confused. Then he smiles. "Oh, I guess I did. Great little pup hanging around in front of the shop. Had to give his ears a scratch or two, didn't I?" He glances toward the hall to the back, ignoring my muttering about the pound. "Is Cassie here? I'd like to include her."

"Nah, it's a gallery day."

"I suppose you don't have to include her in every decision?"

"Depends on what it is."

"It's a business proposition," he says.

I wait for it, one eyebrow cocked, curious. I have no idea what he could propose to me. I'm no businessman. Obviously, if it's about the shop, Cassie would definitely need to be here. It's hers. I just work here. And sometimes sleep on the counter when Cat's in the mood.

He continues, "When you were young, as I recall, you were quite the chef. Your parent's diner was a popular place because of your mother's cooking, and it was still popular when you took over those duties every so often. As you know, I now own the cafe-the Diner of Earthly Delights as it's been renamed..."

"Along with owning pretty much everything else in town." I smile. You have to chop on the guy once in a while. He can be way too serious otherwise.

"Yes. True. And what am I going to do with it when I'm gone? With no heir...." He pauses for a moment, but just a moment. I know he's pushing back grief for his son, Kevin. "With no heir, I've been forced to think very seriously about what I'd like to do with my properties. It's been heartening to see the Giles Gallery back in Dash Simmon's hands. He seems so much more alive now."

I nod. "Cassie says he's like a kid with a new toy. Full of plans for new exhibits with the local artists."

"Yes. I'd like someone to have that level of feeling about the cafe as well. Your father didn't have the heart for it anymore after your mother passed. I know he would have liked to have kept it for you, but...." We don't need to rehash my forty-plus years enslaved as a house cat: nods suffice. He continues, "I'd like to see that put right."

"Put right how?"

"I'm not talking about a gift, Tom. I'm not

Santa Claus. I'm talking about a land lease with sweat equity. You run it, you work it, and we split the profits with a portion of yours going to pay me for the business for a set period of years. How does that sound?"

"It sounds generous...but running the diner?" I let out a low whistle. "A lotta work. I don't know...Cass needs me here."

"That's why I'd hoped to talk to both of you." He puts a hand on my shoulder. "I know that we haven't always been close, but I can't think of anyone I'd rather see end up with the old place. Can you think of someone better suited?"

"Nope." If I had Cat's tail right now, the tip would be tap-tap-tapping with hopeful anticipation. "I'll talk to Cassie."

"Good. We can take up the conversation again after dinner Thursday. Gillian's looking forward to seeing both of you. She apparently has something special planned. Although, with British cookery being what it is, I'm not sure I can fake enthusiasm over it."

"She makes a mean blood pudding," I say.

Robert grins. "There's always delivery." He laughs. "See you then."

It's amazing. Now that there's no one left to keep me down, it just keeps getting better and better. Except for the yapping puppy that jumps at Robert's heels when he leaves the shop. The maddening sound nearly drives the happy from my head, but fortunately, it fades quickly as the noisy pup shadows Robert down the street.

***

Cassie enters from the front of the shop, locking the door behind her. It's closing time now, but I might as well have closed it hours ago. Anyone could have walked off with anything in the shop all day long—probably did—and I wouldn't have noticed. I was planning the diner's new menu in my head, complete with Mother Sander's old style comfort food. Enough of this new-age nonsense. What Giles needs is a stick-to-its-ribs experience.

Before Cass finishes sliding the deadbolt across the door frame, I grab her up in a hug and swing her in a circle. She smacks at my back as she goes around, laughing, and shrieking for me to stop, her long brown hair trailing behind her.

"Tom, stop it, you'll fling me into a shelf and break something!"

Oh sure, she wants to be practical. I set her feet back on the ground and give her an extra-juicy kiss to stifle her laughter and get her in the mood for some serious business talk. Because I'm sure business is always the first thing she thinks of when she's being flung around in circles and tongue-kissed.

I finally release her mouth from mine and pull back to look into her curious blue eyes. I linger there for a while. Yessiree bob, I sure made her forget about the inventory I was supposed to do.

"Okay, so wow!" she says. "I was going to tell you about my weird day at the gallery, but that can wait. Why the crazy-good mood?"

I don't answer for a minute because my eyes are drawn to a flash of movement through the shop door glass. Damn it! That dog is back. And I know I'm paranoid, but I don't like the way it's looking at Cassie. No, my gal only has one furry playmate, and that's me.

I take her hand and lead her back to the kitchenette where no one and nothing can look in on us. I can tell she's dosed on perfume recently, but there's no whiff of dog on her like this morning. Good. "First things first," I say. "I know you. You're starving, I bet." She agrees with me with a "yep" and sits at the table while I hustle up dinner. Something she really likes. Not that I have to put her in a mellow frame of mind—but it couldn't hurt, right?

As I take out the ingredients for a spinach salad and make sure there's still a bowl full of the bacon dressing she likes, ready to be warmed, I say, "Okay, so here's the thing…you know how I love to cook? And that I'm pretty good at it?"

I glance at her, and she looks down at her sexy flat belly, puffing it out and nodding her head. She says, "Yepper, I know."

"So, back when my parents owned the cafe, and

in the rare times when I wasn't running off to do my own thing, I helped them run the place. It was kind of expected that I'd take it over when they wanted to retire. But with me among the missing for so long, well…"

I set a mai tai in front of her. With an umbrella and all. She gives me a look. "Trying to get me drunk?"

"Will it make you more open to suggestion?"

She giggles. "It might. What have you got in mind?"

"Robert wants me to buy the Diner of Earthly Delights, my family's old cafe." She doesn't react at all, and I quickly add, "But not with money. He knows I haven't got any. I'd earn it with my labor. I'd run it, and most of my pay would go toward buying it. It would be back in the family. What do you think?"

She looks disappointed. "That's nowhere near as much fun for me as what I had in mind." Then she beams me a huge grin. Teasing time is over. "But yes, of course you have to do it. Why wouldn't you, if that's what you want?"

I set our salads on the table, then sit down across from her. "With you at the gallery and me at the diner—and it'll be long hours, at least at first—who's going to watch the shop?"

"Don't worry about that!" She reaches across the table with both hands to grasp mine and squeeze them lightly. "I can get someone to work here on my days off. I mean, it would help if that someone is a witch, but it's not absolutely a requirement. I could still prep the magical items and manage the place." She lets go of my hands and places her linen napkin in her lap. "But, yes, it's been easier on me with you already knowing everything about how it runs. But that's not your problem. I completely want you to be happy."

Her baby blues crinkle up a little at the corners as she gives me a huge smile.

The egg timer dings. I pour the now-warm dressing into a jug and push it across to her before it gets cold. "You're amazing. So, I can talk details with Robert when we get together for the weekly dinner?"

"Sure," she says, pouring a little more than her fair share of the dressing onto her plate of greens. "Just try not to be completely boring."

I stand up and move behind her chair, kissing her on the top of the head, and then ease my arms around her. "I think I can find ways to keep your interest. Now, what was it *you* had in mind?"

We race upstairs. Dinner can wait.

TOM WHISPERS he's going to take Cat out hunting and makes an effort not to wake me up too much as he slips out of bed. I wrap up tighter in the warm covers he's just vacated and watch him morph from hot guy to sleek cat, then pad softly into the hall.

Yep. That's my boyfriend, the guy whose passion for canned tuna sometimes borders on obsession. Every so often I like to open a can when he isn't expecting it just to watch his nose twitch until he gets himself back under control.

Seriously. It's adorable. In that weird, welcome-to-my-wacky-paranormal life kind of way, I mean.

I could definitely use some extra sleep this morning before I have to open the shop. We were exhausted last night by the time we fell asleep tangled up in each other. No different than any night, I guess. It's just that every time, it still feels new. Anyway, he never got the chance to go out, and even I can tell Cat needs his me-time. Tom is starting to go all distracted.

When I go downstairs and poke my head in, Cinnamon Kendall, who started going to Salem for her coven meetings after falling out with my granny about ten years ago, is waiting outside the door. Of course, she actually fell out with the demon Anat who'd possessed my granny for most of her life— I'm still rethinking huge chunks of my childhood after finding that out—but she's recently returned to the Giles coven. She's pretty cool, but I'm not letting her in just yet. The shop doesn't even open for another fifteen minutes.

I hope she doesn't see me as I scamper back down the short hall to duck into the kitchenette. I need to get some coffee into me before I can think about a day behind the counter.

While I wait for the old, but still effective, chrome percolator to finish perking my coffee, I clean up last night's dinner. Our salads are still sitting on the table, wilting, giving off a strong scent of onion and honey. I grieve a little for the bacon dressing I'm never going to get to eat.

It's tough to keep my mind where it belongs when it flashes to why I missed my meal. It wants to go back to a warm, Tom-endowed bed.

I sometimes think he and I are a real cliché of young love. Things were never like this when I was with Dan, even though we were only a few months away from being married. He could be sweet, but then he'd turn all critical and mean out of nowhere.

I mean, Tom can be a flake sometimes—I don't know if that's because he has to share his body with a cat or if he's always been that way—but he never gets mean. He's never critical. He loves me exactly as I am. How cool is that?

Sure, Dan was my first love, and I'll probably never forget that. But maybe Tom will be my last. That would be kind of great.

The reminder on my phone goes off with the first notes of "Working Girl". Time to open. No time to daydream about what Tom-and-Cassie kids would look like. And I'd just worked up a pretty picture of a little girl with Tom's soulful brown eyes and my recently-discovered talent for magic.

Oh well. It's show time. I head out to unlock the door.

"Hey Cin, sorry I couldn't open the place early. Had a few things to take care of," I say as I let the waiting witch in.

Cinnamon's bright white teeth flash me a smile that contrasts with her—what does Daria call it when she's being catty? "High yellow" skin tone. Whatever. She's gorgeous, even at forty or so. "S'okay, Cassie. It's a nice day. I was enjoying it." She comes in, trailed by the shiny black puppy I goofed around with the other day. It nips playfully at the hem of her long gypsy-woman skirt.

"Ummm...no pets in the shop. Other than Cat

when he's around, I mean. He's territorial. I'm sorry."

She looks down at the cute little guy behind her. "Not mine. Never seen it. I thought he was yours." She gently pushes it back out the door with one foot.

"So, what can I get you today?"

"I was hoping we both could benefit from an idea I've had. I used to do tarot readings on Tuesday and Thursday nights in the bar at the King of Wands restaurant. But with it closed for the past year, there isn't anywhere people can get a decent glimpse into their future. My only option is once a year during the Witching Faire. I could do readings from my home, but I don't like the idea of having strangers there."

I think about the potential set of strangers you can get going in and out in a town like Giles and bob my head in agreement, "Yeah, I get that."

"I'd be interested in setting up hours in your shop. Just a day or two per week. I'd pay for the floor space, and you'd get extra foot traffic from the ads I run for my services."

It sounds like a great idea. Tourists would eat it up with an ice cream spoon. I idly chomp down on a fingernail while I think about it: she'd need privacy. Then I realize I have a potentially empty room that would be just the thing.

I point toward the back corner of the shop and the short hall that leads to the storage rooms. "The big storeroom would be the right-sized space for a card table and some chairs. The smaller one and the basement storage should be able to cover everything I need to keep on hand these days."

And then I'm wondering what my maybe-babies would look like again. A little glimpse into my own future might be fun. "Maybe a sample of your wares?"

She gives me another brilliant smile. "Of course."

I can't really leave the shop since it's supposed to be open now, and the storeroom still needs to be cleared before it can be made into useful space, so I quickly grab the card table from the parlor closet at the back of the house and plop it in the clear space between the counter and the door. She sits facing the counter while I sit facing the street. She pulls out a deck of old, beautifully inked cards from her purse. Those have got to be handmade. If not, I definitely need some like them for the shop.

My eyes are drawn to the door when I hear a yelp. The pup outside sure is curious. His nose leaves damp impressions on the glass, and he can't take his eyes off of us.

I move my own eyes down to where Cinnamon's placed the deck on the table. She chooses one card and lays it down face up in front of her. It pictures a queen with a staff, sitting on a throne. "I've selected a significator for you. I sense strongly in you all the elements that are represented by the Queen of Wands: warmth, fidelity, and a nurturing personality. But also, there is another side, you see? There. Represented by the cat."

I look closer at the card, and a black cat sits facing the queen. I smirk. That seems about right.

"What does the cat represent on the card?"

"A spirit of independence. And possibly an interest in the occult." Her mouth quirks up at the side as she says that last part.

I look around the shop with a broad taking-it-all-in gesture before I smirk back. "I think you probably nailed it. What's next?"

Her voice drops to a low, melodic tone, "I'll read the Celtic Cross for you. It's an in-depth reading, good for placing the interpretation into the correct context of the past, the present, and the future. If you could shuffle and cut the cards?"

I shuffle, set the deck back on the table, and then lift up about half of the stack and put them to the side. She scoops up both stacks and lays out cards in the shape of a cross around the center significator with others next to it in a line. She places the final card across the center one, face down. I've never had my cards read, and it's interesting to see how it's done. It feels spiritual.

She turns the bottom card in the spread, to reveal an image of a man and woman, their arms around each other, with children at their feet and a rainbow overhead.

"This card represents the basis of the issue—it

symbolizes relationships, romance. Either the beginning of a new partnership or the fulfillment of one already begun. It can mean marriage and family. It's the underlying reason for the reading. The rest of the cards will reference it."

She turns over the card at the left side of the cross and then the one at the right. "Here, you see, just falling away, the Page of Swords. No knight in shining armor for you, but someone who is in a time of renewal, a time of new beginnings. Someone you already know."

"You've met Tom, I think. I'd say that's probably true."

"And here...this is the near future, what is just now coming to be." She pauses, studying the card, then continues, "The ten of swords is a powerful card. It signifies a crisis or a betrayal."

The dog outside starts barking, and the high-pitched sound is kind of irritating. My forehead tenses as I say, "No, that's in the past. It's done with."

"And yet here it is again...." She taps the card with the long painted nail of her right forefinger before her hand moves on to turn over the card on top of the significator. "This card may shed light on that one to tell us if it's an obstacle, a problem to be solved, or someone who is antagonistic to you."

The turn reveals a beautifully drawn woman with a peaceful expression. Another queen, holding a golden cup.

Cinnamon nods her head. "Yes, then it's a betrayal. But one from someone who's your friend, who holds you in esteem. Someone older perhaps, with powerful intuition and a calming influence. But do not think for a moment that she cannot hold the knife when your back is turned."

"Ummm...a friend is going to betray me?" I cross my arms and I know I'm frowning. I glance to the door where the pup's yelps have faded off to a whiny kind of half-bark. Less irritating.

"Yes, so the cards say. But it's only a possibility, something just now coming to be. We'll look at the influences of your house before we seek the outcome." She turns the cards at the right and moves her fingers down them, touching each card in turn, murmuring.

She turns over the top card in the cross and her eyes widen.

She looks up at me, really sucking me in with those big brown eyes of hers that are shadowed with gold and tinged with pity. When I look away, I'm drawn to the puppy at the door again, and I swear their eyes are the same. Big and brown and pitying.

When I turn back to Cinnamon, she says, "Yes, this woman..." she says, pointing to the queen with the cup, "...someone who is involved with your life in a positive way. She will turn on you. You care about her, but you have been jealous of her, too."

Huh. That's not good. She's said nothing about the pretty Tom babies I've been picturing.

"Basically, you're saying my life, which has been pretty good lately, is going to start to suck?"

I hope for a smile or something so we can share in the joke, but she's really flat about it when she says, "Yes, your life will change soon." She points to the card at the top. "This is the Three of Cups, reversed. In the end, there is a third party in your relationship. You must be vigilant to make sure you don't lose everything."

"No way you're talking about Tom, my boyfriend. Someone's going to take him? He's going to cheat on me? No. He isn't like that." And then I remember how he used to be before I knew him. But that was over forty years ago. He's had a lot of time to regret his behavior and get his act together since then. He learned a lot from being trapped in a cat. Which happened because he was cheating on his wife with my granny. Which sounds really bad when I think about it that way. But I'm sticking to my guns. Tom isn't like that. I say, "I mean, he's not like that *now*. Definitely. He's changed."

"The cards are clear on this. You'll be betrayed."

I stand up abruptly. She's just pissing me off now. Basically, she's saying Tom's going to do exactly the same thing to me that my ex-fiancee Dan did.

"Look, I'll call you about the readings, right?" I start folding up the card table to put it away. Maybe I'm a little rough: the legs snap loudly as they clip into their slots. She steps away fast to stay out of my way. I'm not sure I want her doing readings if she's going to give out gloom and doom predictions to the customers. I mean, what woman would want to spend money on lotions and potions when she's just been told her boyfriend is going to go off with another woman?

But mine's not. Definitely and completely not. I don't think Cinnamon knows anything about reading the cards, after all.

As she leaves, that pup finds its moment and sneaks in, nearly making her trip as he slips under her skirt and between her legs in a rush. And then he's there in front of me, staring up at me with those big, brown, pitying eyes. It feels...personal. Like he's telling me he's here for me. That he understands.

Yep, after a dire reading like that one, I really do need some puppy love. But Tom is going to kill me if he finds out this dog is in the shop. I bend and pick it up. As I carry it out, I hold it away from my body so it can't give me a slurp. When we get outside, I set it down gently, giving it a soft push on its way before I shut the door behind it.

**

I hear a low moan, and an "ouch" floats down the hall from the parlor, alerting me that my Tomcat is back from his hunt. Tom's transformation is always painful, but he says he owes a lot to Cat and doesn't want to coop him up all the time. Plus, it's not pretty when the Cat starts to take over the man.

I'm not sure how it all works, but I have no problem with his hunting expeditions. It's kind of his version of boy's night out. And anyway, Cat is part of our lives. Tom's needing to shift every so often is our normal. It's no big deal.

No big deal. Wow. My concept of reality sure has changed since Granny Eunice died and I was introduced to the supernatural world she hid from me.

I hope I've wiped off all evidence of doggy visitors so that I'm not in for a lecture. I scrubbed the cheek where the pup kissed me for at least five minutes just to make sure.

My cleansing efforts must have been effective. Strong arms slip around my waist from behind and snug me up tight. I never hear him coming: he really is stealthy as a cat. I tingle all over when he pushes my hair aside. First his warm breath, and then his lips, graze my neck. He smells musky, still wearing our night of love-making.

"Stop it! You're such a tease. You know I have to work!" I pivot to him, leaning against the counter and raising my arms to hug him around his broad shoulders without ever breaking the body contact between us.

He smiles down at me. "Close the shop. You need a vacation."

We separate a little. Not a lot. Just enough so we can see each other's faces while we talk. I'm not letting go just yet. "And who will put food on your table if I blow off all my duties?" I ask.

"Oh, I see how it is." He grins. "Well, pretty soon, I'll be putting the food on your table. On a whole bunch of tables. I can't stop thinking about the diner. I had no idea I'd want it this much."

I raise a hand to the side of his face. He looks so darn sweet all lit up with excitement about getting his family's business back. How could anyone even suggest this guy would run around on me?

"Do you think it's legal for two people to be so happy?" I ask.

"Probably not. We're criminals, the two of us. Lo-o-ove criminals."

It sounds stupid, but I can't help it. I laugh anyway.

"Hey…Cinnamon Brown, you know her?" He nods, and I continue, "She was in here earlier because she wants to set up to do tarot readings from the shop, and I couldn't resist getting a free reading, but…" I stop, thinking of what I should tell him about it. There's no reason he should feel bad. He hasn't done anything.

His eyes seek mine out, appraising my expression. "She said something that rattled you."

I shrug. "It was just dumb, I guess. She had the past and the present pegged, but when she told me about my future, well…she suggested that there would be loss and betrayal—that basically, my lover was going to man-whore around on me, and I had to be careful or I could lose everything."

His brows furrow as he says, "Really? And which lover is that, because it sure ain't me—you're stuck with me, babe." His hand moves under my chin and gently lifts my face to his. "Man, if you don't know that by now, how can I ever convince you?"

I melt. I always melt when he gets that look. The look that says I'm the best thing he's ever seen, his eyes dilated and boring straight into mine. Who could fake that look? What else can I say but, "Yeah, dumb, right?"

He pulls me in for a long, reassuring kiss, his lips soft and warm against mine like they were made just for me. Why did I even give that stupid reading one milli-moment of thought? This guy fought and defeated a demon for me! How could I doubt him?

Then, his fingers pull in like claws across my back and disrupt the caress. He lets out a long "ssssss" right by my ear.

I push him away and look up at him, surprised. "Was that a hiss?"

He nods, and his eyebrows lift. He looks just as weirded out as I feel. "Cat took over for a minute. Instinct." He chins toward the door. "There's a dog looking in the window. And Cat doesn't like the looks of him one bit."

I turn, and he's right. The pup is back. "I think

he's cute," I say. "Are you sure Cat doesn't want a playmate?"

"Cat and I already have our best possible playmate."

He pulls me close again, and I don't even pretend to resist him.

***

A couple of regulars come in, and Tom and I can't stand around necking like teenagers anymore. I break away from him with a promise for later. Work to do.

He starts on the inventory down in the basement. I keep an eye on the customers while I bag loose teas, grind herbs, and create charms. There's a workspace at the counter specifically for that. The customers enjoy watching the "magic" being created, although the out-of-towners are more amazed by the faint glow at my fingertips that adds the magic to the charms than the locals are.

Funny how you can use magic right out in public and no one questions it. The people who believe in magic would believe it even if it was smoke and mirrors, and the ones who believe that it is smoke and mirrors still get a kick out of it while they try to figure out how it's done. So, I've decided why bother keeping it in the back room anymore, right? It's a draw.

There's a little guy maybe five or six years old

with a bright, eager gleam in his eyes standing in front of the counter, watching me select the stones for an amulet. We have a supplier who sends the ones with natural holes. A drilled hole just isn't the same: it won't hang on to the magic that gives the wearer good luck and protection. Once I've strung a few of them onto a leather cord and hold it up to make sure it's aesthetically pleasing, I pass my hand over it, intoning, "For luck, for love, for pleasant things; Be safe, be strong in your wanderings."

Then I pass a little touch of my magic to the amulet like a mini lighting bolt. Flashy, I know. But the kid's eyes get big and round and his mouth turns into a perfect O for just a second. I lean across the counter and hand it to him.

"If you wear this, it will bring you good luck and keep you safe."

He grabs it and runs to his mother who's paging through the spell books, holding it out for her to see. "And it really is magic, mom...'lectricity came from the lady's fingers..."

"Put it back, dear. We're not buying any geegaws today."

I walk over. "No, it's a gift." I crouch down and take it from him to slip it over his head, but I hold off with it in position while I look to his mom for permission. "Everybody can use a little extra luck, right?"

She looks unsure, then says, "Okay. But thank the lady, Jimmy," after deciding I'm probably not some crazed child molester.

After I straighten the stones across his small chest and stand up, he says, "Thank you, lady," and grabs me around the legs with a big hug as his mother turns back to her browsing. I pat him on the head and then head back toward the counter. Cute kid.

Tom is standing behind the register when I join him, he says, "I bet you'd be an amazing mother."

I smile. What can I say? It's not like I haven't been thinking about nesting pretty much constantly for the past couple of weeks. But there's plenty of time, and what Tom and I have is still so new. I say, "Maybe I should start practicing with a pet. You know, like a puppy."

He rolls his eyes up and inclines his head, putting one finger up to his mouth in an exaggerated "let me think" pose and shifts his eyes slightly in another direction every couple of seconds for emphasis. He keeps it up so long that I can't help but giggle and say, "Okay, okay. No puppies."

But the pup with the wet, black nose pressed up against the door glass is at it again when I turn my attention back to charm making, and well...he's awfully cute. I'm sure Cat could get used to him. Because I already kind of feel like he's mine, like he's meant for me.

"OMIGOD, YOU GUYS are so adorable together!"

Daria squees at the selfie I made with Tom this morning.

"I know, right? He's gorgeous." I take my phone back and have to look at the pic for a second myself. "You have to come by the shop and meet him. He's the best."

"What? Even think about walking in to that shop of yours? If my mama finds out about that, she'll snatch me bald, girl. And you know I'll never be so old I'll stop being afraid of my mama."

I give her a broad grin as I think about her mother's stern look over the top of crimson-rimmed glasses that ride low on her nose when she's deciding whether or not you're in trouble. "Nobody will ever be so old that they'll stop being afraid of your mama."

"Your granny wasn't afraid. You ever wonder what went on between those two that got my mama so bent out of shape?"

"Granny Eunice was a special case." Boy was she ever. I'm still sorting it all out in my head—who my real granny was if you strip away all the bad stuff Anat made her do. I think she must have been very brave. I know she fought back against Anat in ways I couldn't when Anat possessed me after Granny died. I wish I'd been able to know Eunice for who she really was. But it's too late. I break out of my reverie and say, "Okay, if you can't come by the shop, then let's all have dinner some time. You can bring a date."

"Like you haven't locked up the only guy over 18 and under 40 who lives within the city limits."

"That's true—you don't see many guys our age around." I don't straighten her out about Tom actually being in his seventies like his friend Robert. Except he's not, not in any real way. It's confusing.

"Mmmm hmmm, and guys our age in chocolate? Nope. I should do what my cousin Keisha did—found herself a job with some rich white guy. Can you believe he gave her a house when he laid off? How crazy is that? She swears every which way all she ever did was clean the house and have a glass of wine with him once in a while. Like she's gonna convince me of that."

I make horselips, blowing air out between them

like I'm totally with her. "Pretty crazy."

But I know all about it. And I still hope Keisha never finds out about Kevin's secret visits to her bathroom window while dressed up in the invisibility suit my granny—no, *Anat*—made for him. I know its wrong to be glad he's dead, but I am. Sucking his life-force out was the one thing that evil-demon bitch goddess did right.

"Look," I say, giving a quick glance down to the time on my phone. "I've gotta go, but as possibly the only still-single representatives of our generation left in Giles, we need to get together more often."

We stand and hug, and she replies, "You got it, girl. And I want to meet that hot guy of yours, see if I can steal him away." She laughs, but the insecure part of me that can't stop thinking about that stupid tarot reading catches and gives a tug at my heart.

***

The pup is sneaking around the trash cans, pushing at the lid of one with the tip of his nose, when I cruise up the alley into the parking space behind the shop. He really must not have anywhere to go, even though he looks pretty well fed for a stray. Still, I don't need him knocking the cans over and making a mess.

"Hey, stay away from those! There's no dinner for you in there," I shout, stepping out of the car before he can do any damage. He looks up, and if a dog's face can look like it's glad to see me, his does. His ears perk up, and I swear he smiles.

Then he comes scampering toward me and jumps up to put his muddy little paws on my clean jeans. He smells like he's had some success at someone's garbage—I get just the tiniest whiff of rotting meat covered by the stronger smell of gardenia—but I can't get mad, can I? He's so darn cute.

I look down at him, knowing I'm smiling like a goof but trying to look super serious. "For real, you need to take off before the cat gets back. He's a mean one. A little guy like you wouldn't stand a chance." And I mean that, too. Cat could take him. He's one fearless feline.

The back door opens and Tom appears in the doorway. The pup turns tail and runs off without a single look back.

"Damn that dog! He already spilled the cans once today and managed to get into the house while I was cleaning up the mess because I forgot to latch the door. It took me forever to catch him and get him back outside. He was all the way upstairs, wreaking havoc."

Tom responds poorly to my manipulative cut-the-little-guy-a-break expression. "Oh no, don't use that face on me! If that dog moves in, Cat and I will be moving out. You have no idea what dog smells like until you've experienced dog stink through a cat's nose."

I don't even know how to argue with that. I reply, "Do you see me bringing him in? I'm not bringing him in."

"Well, okay," he says. "As long as you're not bringing him in." He raises one eyebrow way up his forehead and inclines that side of his head toward me. "But you know I'll have to keep an eye on you, right? Night and day, probably."

I give him a tiny eye roll. "Well, if you have to." We grab for each other at the same time, laughing.

***

Tom heads for the kitchen to start dinner and I make my way upstairs to get rid of my heels and into something comfortable to lounge around in after we eat.

Our bed is unmade, which is weird because I know I made it this morning. Granny drilled it into me to make the bed the second I got out of it, and I took that habit home with me after the first time I stayed with her. It's not something I forget. Tom wouldn't have come up for a nap. It was his long day in the shop.

Oh well, maybe I did forget. But I sure can't leave it like this. I pull the spread back and start to straighten the sheets...and no way!

I reach out for the foreign object in the bed, and it's a pair of women's panties. A large, not-at-all sexy pair of women's white cotton panties. Granny panties. What the hells?

I hold them up in front of me at their full width, and the only thing I can think of is that these are just about Gillian's size.

That thing that catches inside me and tugs at my heart? It's tugging like mad. I'm surprised my heart even goes on beating.

"Tom?" I yell. I try not to sound frantic. This isn't what it looks like. It can't be.

"Cass? You okay?" he responds, his voice rising up the stairwell.

"No," I manage to get out before my throat closes up.

He slams up the stairs and is in the doorway before a tear has time to fall.

"Cass?" He stands there looking at me holding up the gigantic panties, the expression on his face all concern. But is it concern for me or concern that he just got caught?

"Whose are these?" I ask, forcing my voice not to quiver.

He shakes his head. "I don't know. But I'll play. Whose are they?"

I have to hand it to him, he looks genuinely surprised. "They were in our bed."

"Well, they're not mine. Not even close to the right size or style. You know that better than anyone, since you helped pick out all my modern clothes." He turns his hands up in an "I dunno" gesture. I mean, if he's acting, he's good.

"Well, I know they're not mine. So how did they get here?"

Then he catches on. "You're not really thinking.... That I?" His eyes broadcast alarm. "I would never do anything like that to you. Never."

He comes toward me with his arms out to hold me, but I stiff-arm him with the wall o' undies.

It doesn't shut him up, though. "Look, Cass, when would I even have time to lure another woman into our bed? This morning I made you breakfast and then you took off for Boston to shop. After that, I stopped to see Darrin at the animal hospital because Cat managed to get himself stung by something that has one of his paws swollen up. And then I did the laundry and had to take everything over to the laundromat because the dryer has given up the ghost, and then I put all that stuff away and tidied up, and then I worked in the shop, and then I had to clean up after that stupid mutt turned the upstairs into a mess and chase him around to get him out of the house. I maybe had ten minutes in between that and when you got home."

When he says it that way, I kind of feel like maybe the guy's a little henpecked. And then it hits me. "What did you take to the laundry?"

"The parlor curtains, the sheets, a bunch of my stuff, and those jeans that look so hot on you."

I let out a huge breath. Wow. That stupid tarot reading is really doing me in. It makes sense now.

"So, these probably got left in the dryer and stuck to the sheets when you took them out."

"Whew. Can I just say I'm glad you solved the mystery before you threw me out? Although I'm surprised I didn't find them when I made the bed. I was in a hurry, I guess. It took a lot longer to drag all the stuff over there and wait around for it to be ready than I thought it would. Didn't have a lot of time before the shop opened when I got back." He grabs the undies out of my hands and drops them in the trash. "Look, I have a nice dinner down there that isn't going to make itself. Are we good?"

"Yeah, we're good. Sorry." And then I remember the part about Darrin, our friend who uses his healing magic as a vet. "Cat's okay, right?"

"He's good. Darrin did some mumbo jumbo healing touchy-feely and gave me a salve to dunk the paw in if it gets worse."

He kisses me and then he's down the stairs. I take just a little bit longer to collect myself before I follow him. I have to stop thinking about that reading.

But wait a minute. If he made the bed, why was it messed up again? No, no. I'm not going there. Both Tom and Gillian love me. They wouldn't. I know they wouldn't.

Unless—my puppy? Oh sure—a cute little puppy messed up the bed and left some big girl's underpants in it because he's trying to break us up.

Yeah, that reading has definitely made me crazy.
No, it's like Tom said, they came in on the laundry.
   I'm sure they did.

I KEEP A STEALTHY eye out on the middle-aged couple who are admiring the watercolors at the back of the gallery. I can only pretend to be fascinated by the flyers I'm folding for so long. I don't want to hover, but I also don't want to miss a sale because I let them walk away with unfulfilled desire in their eyes.

The watercolors are an especially nice group by a Boston artist who paints in Giles during the summer. Dash would never have a pastel landscape in the shop; these are bold, aggressive works with just a touch of nature's violence. Thinking about it, I'd say that just about sums up my own last summer in Giles.

Dash comes in from the back, where's he's been spending a lot of time in his bolt hole lately, with or without Jon. I don't even want to know what that's about. Whatever's been going on, he's not his usual flamboyant self, that's for sure. But when I ask, he says everything is okay.

But even without his normally joyful spirit, he's still an amazing salesmen. He would never push a piece of art to someone who wouldn't love it, but the second he spots the look of love between a painting and a customer, he's all over it until he's got them mated up and living happily ever after.

I can only hope to be that good some day. I mean, who doesn't want to put a painting into the hands of someone who will love it rather than someone who's looking for an investment or something with cool factor to cover a blank spot on the wall?

I ready myself to move in on the woman because she has "the look" as she gives one of the landscapes the once-twice-thrice over. Oh yeah, those two definitely want to go home together tonight.

As I start to move in, Dash glances at me, sees me heading in for the close, then heads for the couple before I go a second step.

Wow. That's not like Dash. That was just mean.

What's going on with him?

I need air.

***

It's times like this that I wish I smoked so I

don't look so conspicuous just hanging out, leaning against the building, taking a break. Dash smokes, so I come out with him sometimes when there aren't any customers.

We like to people-watch. It's fun. And Dash can dish. He knows practically everybody, and the people he doesn't know, he's heard all the gossip about anyway. He's such an old biddy sometimes. I love it, though.

There's not a lot of people out on the street. It's starting to get chilly, especially at night. But Halloween—or Samhain, really—I guess I better get used to the witch name for the holiday—is still close to two weeks away, and Giles doesn't usually get wintry before then. If it does, it pretty much wrecks the annual Witching Faire.

Weather here can be a little whacked sometimes, even more in the spring than in the fall. But most years, Giles definitely gets snow by Christmas. Not that Granny celebrated it. But the town center was always lit up awfully nice.

Once Halloween—Samhain, I mean—is over, I have to ask Tom to dig out the Christmas decorations and take an inventory of what we've got when he's done putting the Halloween ones away. Granny never did much with decorations. She'd maybe put some black tinsel garlands in the window and fresh evergreen boughs on the shelves near the ceiling with the canopic jars. That smelled nice. But she just hinted at it.

I want a big-deal Christmas blowout with all the trimmings, which will be a first in that old house and the shop. And presents. I completely insist on presents. Lots and lots of presents.

The black pup that's been hanging around the shop comes snuffling toward me, nose low to the sidewalk, but when he looks up and sees me, he bounds toward me gleefully.

"You'd want a fancy Christmas at the shop, wouldn't you, boy?" I say, as I squat down with my back against the wall to pet him.

Thinking about the shop, I glance down the street, and…what the heck?

Tom is getting out of Gillian's car. And he didn't just step in there for a minute for some gossip. He has to unlock the shop door before he can go in.

They went somewhere together secretly when he was supposed to be working? I reach down and cuddle the pup, looking deeply into those understanding eyes of his. It's comforting that he's here, now that I know for a fact that Tom has been sneaking around with Gillian.

I WAVE BACK to Gillian before I close the door. With me not having a driver's license since the sixties, her offer to chauffeur me to Boston really helped me out.

After I slip the shop keys back into my pocket, I check my wallet for the tenth time since we left the store to make sure the receipt is still in there. The all-important receipt.

The receipt that will make my last dream come true.

The receipt that puts a ring on Cassie's finger.

If she accepts it, I'll be the one getting the world's best Christmas gift, not her. That's why I was glad Gillian went with me—I needed someone to make sure the I got the right kind of ring, the kind Cassie would want to wear. Me? I'd probably pick out the biggest, gaudiest thing just because of the sparkles. Someone had to come with me who wouldn't succumb to cat brain when presented with shiny things.

The stone isn't much because I can't afford much. But the setting I picked is elegant, and Gillian approved. She's sure that Cassie will love it.

The shop bell rings, and I turn, expecting to greet a customer, but it's Cass. I grin automatically. She has that effect on me, but my mood dampens when the annoying stray puppy that's been hanging around trails in behind her before the door closes.

Cassie's blue eyes are narrowed into a thin line, and her candy-pink lips are pressed together tight. She's definitely not grinning back.

"Baby? Is something wrong?"

"You lied to me, Tom. You lied!" She moves toward me and slams me in the chest with the flat of her hands twice before I manage to capture them and hold them still. She struggles against me. The pup sits still behind her, watching. "You said you'd never treat me the way you treated Gillian, and yet that's who you're sneaking around with."

I feel like I've been punched in the gut. "Cass, what are you talking about? The panties? You know those came in on the sheets from the Laundromat. I thought we'd gotten past that."

"You snuck off with Gillian when you were supposed to be working. I saw you get out of her car. Did you return her underwear while you were with her?"

Great. I've been rumbled. And I can hardly say I haven't been sneaking around with Gillian when I have. I force myself to stay calm, talk softly, and hold her marauding hands as gently as I can to prevent any further damage.

I'm way too aware of the dog that followed her in. It's too distracting to stay. When I'm not Cat, I haven't even got hackles, but everything in me still wants to raise them.

"You've got it wrong, babe. I know how it looks, but Gillian gave me a ride to Boston as a favor. I can't tell you what I was shopping for." She backs away from me, not struggling anymore, so I let go of her hands. I move around her as I talk then, bending to grab the dog by the scruff of the neck, open the shop door, and slide it out, letting the door slam behind it.

With my focus back, I turn to Cassie. "It would ruin the surprise if I told you where we went. There's no place to get the Christmas gift I'm getting you in Giles, and I don't have a driver's license, remember?"

Her tight, angry face relaxes a little. "It's not even Halloween yet. Why are you shopping for Christmas?"

"Like I don't know it's your favorite day of the year? I want our first Christmas together to be special. I want to surprise you. So I had to get a ride from *someone*."

She looks at me, appraising. She's still prickly,

not ready to forgive me just yet. The pup whines from outside, paws on the door, peering in.

I lunge toward it, baring my teeth and wishing I could whip my fangs out.

"Tom, leave the poor thing alone!" Cassie makes a face at me, but the lunge worked. The dog trots away. She watches it go, then says, "Why Gillian?"

"It's a very..." I stretch for words that won't give it away but might explain my choice of driver and continue with, "...feminine gift. Robert wouldn't be much help, and Natalie would be worse. Unless you want a red handbag and matching go-go boots?"

She looks curious now. "How feminine? I sure wouldn't want Gillian picking out my lingerie."

"No guessing! It's a surprise. Unless it's the only way for me to get back on your good side?" I keep up a brave front here, but inside, I hate it. I want to go down on one knee right now. Why put it off? But I know why. Because Cassie loves Christmas, and I want to make it her best one ever. I know she feels about me the way I do about her. It will be the right time. I'm sure of it.

"I...I..." I can tell she's softening.

I take my final shot. "It would ruin what I have planned for Christmas. I mean, really ruin it."

She takes a deep breath, looking into my eyes unwaveringly, searching.

I say, "But I'll ruin it, if I have to, so that you'll believe me."

Her face works through a cycle of emotions as she thinks it over. But none of them are the angry, jealous one she wore when she walked in with that pup. Then she puts a hand on my shoulder. "I'm sorry. It just looked…"

"I know. I'm sorry, too. I promise I won't sneak around with my ex again. I'll have to go into Boston one more time, but I'll let you know when we're going."

"Okay," she says. And then she gasps, fully back to normal. "I'm supposed to be working. Dash is going to kill me!"

She turns and runs out. She doesn't see the stray pup as it lopes back into the doorway, and she nearly creams it when she flings the door open. It jumps back out of danger in the nick of time. The little creep just can't stay away from her. Maybe it's just me reacting to Cat's thoughts on the matter, but I don't like that pooch one bit.

He frolics after her as she hurries away.

***

Things weren't normal between us last night when Cassie came home from the gallery, and she didn't want to talk about it. Nothing puts me on the alert more than when a woman doesn't want to talk about her feelings. Not that I could bring it up. No. Nothing to do but wait it out.

Plus, that dog was following her. I swear I hate

that dog. If I really tried, I bet I could get an obsession with clearing up the stray dog population going again.

She watched some TV and said she was going to bed. I got a good night kiss, but it was a peck. An afterthought. I was sure we'd talk it out tonight, and then have great make-up sex like we did the night of the Great Panty Incident, but we didn't make love for the first time since her last moonblood.

I can't just lay here watching Cassie breathe, willing her to wake up with a smile to let me know that she's not still angry, so I take Cat out for an early morning hunt.

I guess if I was a girl who was with me, I'd worry, too. But there's no reason. The cheating Tom that got himself turned into a tomcat is long gone. I'm a one-woman man now. And Cassie is that one woman for me.

The hunt is less satisfying than usual. My thoughts crowd Cat's out and his reactions are off. When he launches himself in his first attempt at breakfast, he misses his mousey prey by a whisker. My fault. It's a good thing Cat's not much of one for assigning blame.

As I pad back to the house, we lick our lips to get the last of the blood from the mole we finally caught, despite my ruminating, disposed of before he goes in. Wise move. Cassie doesn't like to see evidence of his predatory nature. She likes to pretend that things around Giles are nice and civilized. I guess it helps her feel safe.

A metallic crash sounds when I glide through the slats of the neighbor's fence beside the back driveway behind the shop. I stop halfway through, wary, the instinct to avoid danger kicking in hard. I hunker down, surveying my surroundings, ready for fight or flight.

That damn dog! He's knocked over a trash can again, spilled the contents, and grabbed up the underwear that got all of the mess between me and Cassie going in the first place.

That's it. Cat's going to war. Hackles rise, claws extend, and my ears skim back flat across my head.

I go in with teeth and claws blazing.

The pup yelps as Cat's claws rake across it's sensitive nose. It snaps at me, but I'm way too fast for it. I'm around behind and jump across it's back, fixing my teeth into one of its stupid, floppy ears. The smell is wretched. Dogs. Yuck. But I'm doing some serious damage.

It tries to shake me off, but I only release my grip by a fraction to swiftly get a better one.

And then I react to a swick across my backside with the business end of a broom, and I let go, more than surprised.

Cassie took a broom to me?

"In the house. And don't even try to explain this to me."

Right at the moment, I think it's best to do as I'm told.

I hear her cooing and soothing the pup as Cat stalks away to follow her instructions. I'd say Cat's pride is wounded, but that would be a lie. Cat doesn't care. He knows there will be plenty of time later on to murder that broom over and over.

When she finally comes back in, I'm dressed and waiting in the kitchen for her in the pajama pants I dashed upstairs to grab, working on her favorite cinnamon-dusted french toast for an apology breakfast. "Look, I'm sorry. But Cat's a cat. And that dog made a mess with the trash again."

"He's a helpless little puppy, Tom. And I know we can't take him in because of Cat, but if you let Cat attack him like that one more time..."

I flip the toast briskly to dust the other side. "I can't seem to get anything right for the past few days." I don't look at her when I say it, and I don't turn when she responds.

"I don't know why I'm overreacting to everything, either. I'm sorry," she says.

Okay, now I can turn and still be manly. She's admitted there's a problem between us so I don't have to. I flop her breakfast onto a blue ceramic plate, top it with a huge pat of butter, and set it in front of her.

She looks down at her breakfast, approving, as she picks up her fork and turns her eyes back to me. She continues, "But I'm kind of glad we've had our first fight—really our first two fights, I guess. Aren't you? I mean, things will always be more complicated for us than other people—witch and werecat and all that—but I'm not sure why every little thing is setting me off."

She gets up and slides around me suddenly, and opens the fridge, leaving her breakfast untried. That isn't like her. She should be shoveling it in by now. She stares in at the fridge contents for a minute. "What do you think a puppy would like to eat?"

"You're feeding it?" I work to keep the frustration out of my voice.

"It won't have to dump over people's garbage cans if it's getting enough to eat."

Maybe she's right. But it intentionally went for those panties. It's trying to break us up.

Right. And now who's overreacting?

***

I look over when the shop door opens just before closing time, and it's Robert. Good. I'm tired of new age housewives today, to tell the truth. I extricate myself from the one I'm explaining the healing properties of amethyst to and go to greet him.

"What brings you in, Robert?"

"I need a jolt of that herbal painkiller I use for my arthritis. It's almost effective, and I need to stay limber, what with Gillian around, expecting me to get into the strangest positions."

"What is it they say these days, Robert? Too

much information?"

"Yoga, Tom, yoga!"

I shrug. "Of course. Exactly what I was thinking. I'll just go grab those pills."

As I ring up the sale, he asks, "Did you talk to Cassie about the diner?"

"She's all for it. We can talk about it tonight."

"After dinner, yes. It's an excellent excuse to have a brandy, send the girls to the kitchen to do the dishes, and talk business. That should go over well."

We grin at each other. Neither one of us minds that we will more likely discuss it over the dishes while our partners retire to the study to add to Cassie's store of knowledge about magic. They meet a couple of times a week, but Cassie wants as much time learning as she can get. She's already mastered Gillian's specialty of magical breaking and entering, and now they've gone on to wards and protection. She says she never wants to have to feel helpless again. With our recent history, I don't see a single reason to protest.

I walk Robert to the door and we grasp hands in a goodbye shake. "See you in a few hours, then," he says.

"Natalie's not coming tonight?" Cassie asks as we sit down to dinner. "I was looking forward to seeing her."

"I'm afraid not, dear," Gillian says, as she sets a huge roast surrounded by artfully arranged vegetables down on the middle of the table. "She's a little put out with us right now, but she'll get over it." Then she takes her seat next to Robert and glances to him, looking giddy and girlish. "We have an announcement."

"Yes, indeed we do." He smiles and places his hand over hers on the table. "Gillian and I have decided to live in sin as a full time thing." He squeezes her hand, and then continues. "Truthfully, she never quite moved out after the Anat fiasco, but it's ridiculous that she has to keep running over to her place to look after Polly, so she's bringing the bird along, too, and we're making it official. Neither one of us has enough time left that we want to waste any of it."

Cassie jumps up and runs over to grab Gillian around the neck in an enthusiastic hug. Robert and I stand to enjoy a manly round of back-patting and hand-shaking. Also enthusiastic.

I'm glad for both of them. They deserve to be happy. It's easy to see that they are. Maybe not stars-in-their-eyes in love like me and Cassie, but you can see the glow between them.

Dinner and the company are both pleasant. Cassie sometimes wishes we had more friends our age, and I don't remind her that Gillian, Robert and Nat *are* my age. But I get her point.

After dinner, the girls take off to do their thing, and Cassie's giggle wafts in from the living room every so often as Robert and I talk. I don't think it's the magic that's got them so wound up. And I'm glad Cassie has proof now that there's absolutely no way that anything would be going on between me and Gillian. I mean, what more proof could she want? Gillian is all smiles every time Robert looks at her.

After we guys wash the dishes, just like I'd predicted, Robert goes into his study and comes back with two cigars, already trimmed and ready to be lit. He inclines his head toward the back door. "New rules, I'm afraid. No stinking cigars in the house." He sighs. "Women!" But he's still got a smile on his face.

We don our jackets and head for the back deck, where we sink into a couple of chairs and Robert throws a blanket over his knees to keep them warm against the evening chill. A black pup comes bounding up the deck's stairs and jumps onto his lap like he's expected. "You again?" he says, scratching its ears. "I'm sure I told you that I can't have a dog now that I'm going to have a Polly. You need to go home where you belong."

"We've got one just like him hanging around the shop. Nasty little thing. Can't be the same one, though."

"I wouldn't expect so. This fellow's too young to travel that far. He's sure a nice one. Has some Lab in him, I'd guess," he says, scratching at the dog's ears. "I had one like him when I was young. If it weren't for Gillian moving in, I think this pup might have found himself a home. I need to put some effort into finding out where he belongs, I suppose. I couldn't stand to see him ending up at the pound." He looks at me pointedly.

"Look, my days of turning in strays to the pound are done. I got the one I needed, so now it's live and let live." I've actually started to feel a little guilty about my stray dog clearing adventures a few months ago. It doesn't stop me from glaring at the pup, though. "I have to tell you, despite wishing it no harm, I'm not happy to be so close to it."

Robert looks at me a little sharply for such an

innocuous comment. Then he raises his eyebrows and relaxes them, his expression normal again. "I guess that makes sense, given the circumstances."

"It's instinct. Cat's. Not mine. I had a dog or two of my own back in the day. But now? They just make me want to hiss and spit."

"Glad to see you're restraining yourself." He sets the dog down and gives it a push in the direction of the stairs. "Go on, go home. There's no place for you here, boy."

I watch the dog disappear into the darkness at the edge of the yard.

And then, oh dear Goddess, please let that be a possum: for the briefest moment, I'm looking into a pair of glowing red eyes.

I bolt out of my chair and run toward the two spots of red.

They wink out before I reach them.

***

"I saw it, Robert! Don't try to calm me down. It was that dog, the one from the ritual grounds. The one that Anat took over. She must have gotten out of the pound somehow. These pups, they must be hers. She'll never, ever leave me alone."

Robert stays calm. Robert always stays calm. "Tom, it's been quiet for a couple of months. And you yourself made sure she got what she deserved. If she could do anything to you, even if she did survive the pound, don't you think she would have tried something already?"

"How would I know? Why did Anat ever do anything? It was all just on a whim with her."

"I'm only suggesting that I don't think there's a reason for alarm. Anat depended a lot on the power of the witch she possessed and the power she could steal from others within the choir. We know that now, and we didn't before. I don't think a dog has what it takes to power her magic."

"Do you know how happy I am right now, Robert? And how much Anat would love to interfere with that? I mean, don't say anything to Cassie, but I've bought a ring, and I'm going to get down on one knee and beg her to marry me soon."

A smile splits his face from ear to ear. "She's going to make an honest man out of you, then? Good for the both of you!"

"But don't you see? It won't happen. Because that bitch—and she is, literally now, a bitch—will never, ever let me have that kind of happiness."

"Do you want to talk to the girls about it? Get their take? I think you're being paranoid, but if you want another opinion..."

I think about it and realize that if Robert's alarm bells aren't going off, then maybe I'm going to wreck everyone's celebration tonight for no reason. He suffered because of her, too. She took his son. He wouldn't just shrug it off if he thought there was a possibility what I'm saying has merit.

I shake the anxiety. "No. Not while everyone's so happy. I can't."

And he's right. I know he's right. Anat picked both Eunice and Cassie so she'd have access to their power. She wouldn't have picked a non-magical, and she definitely wouldn't have picked a dog if she'd had any other choice. "I'm sure you're right. And what's a dog going to do to me, anyway? Sniff my crotch to death?"

***

When we go back into the house, our filthy cigars extinguished and the agreement about the diner made, Cassie beams at me. "Gillian agreed to manage the shop if Natalie will help. I think this can work, don't you?"

No, I'm not mentioning my stupid fears to her when she's so full of glow. This will allow her to spend more of her energies on the art she loves. I probably didn't see anything at all out there. Cassie and I have been through a lot recently. I'll keep my paranoia to myself.

I go to her and put my arms around her, glad to have her this close, wanting to get her home to make up for what we missed last night. Robert has his arms around Gillian, and they're looking into each other's eyes as well, thinking the same thing I bet.

Oh goddess, I didn't need to think about that.

That cools my jets a little. A lot. Now I've got this picture of Robert and Gilly going at it like a couple of amorous weasels stuck in my head. Someone needs to knock me unconscious right now.

I distract myself by asking, "Would you be able to start next week, Gilly? I'd love to get into the diner as quickly as possible. Start planning for the holiday menu, that kind of thing. I'm thinking about taking the offerings back to old fashioned comfort food but with a modern twist."

She smiles and says, "I think there are a lot of older residents in Giles who'd welcome a change from the foody nonsense that's been going on there for the past few years, don't you, Robert?"

"Yes, I do. I remember Tom's mother's cooking very fondly. And, as I recall, there were some quite good senior prices?"

Here I am at Robert's huge mansion of a house with its wood, leather, and elegant old brick, and I just have to shake my head. He's a skinflint to the core, like a lot of our generation in this state. He wants to save his buck on lunch even though he's worth a bundle. But I guess that makes it even more generous what he's doing for me with the diner. "Yes, there were. And maybe there will be again—or just a discount for special friends."

They walk us to the door, and I wave goodbye as Cassie backs the car down the drive. I'm happy for them.

But my thoughts aren't on the happy couple any

more when I'm sure I catch a flash of red glinting in the bushes before we're out on the open road.

Paranoia. That's all it is.

WHEN GILLIAN SAID she'd love to work at the store the when Tom and I had dinner at their place, I was over the moon. I'm even more over the moon now that it's two days later, she's here for her first day of work, and she's brought Natalie with her. I guess they've patched things up—either that, or Nat isn't going to let Gillian increase her influence in the witching community by managing the shop on her own. Whatever the reason, it takes a huge load off my shoulders with Tom heading for his first day at the diner this morning. I just need to remind them of a few things before I leave them alone and take off myself for the gallery.

"Okay, so...you guys know where most things are, but I don't think either one of you have been down in the basement where we keep some of the non-perishables or into the storeroom where we have a little work area for things that can't really be prepared on the workspace at the counter. You won't need either of those areas today, so I'll give you a better orientation before you do. The biggest thing is no mammal parts—like the fetal pig for your lotion, Nat—should ever be on display in a customer area without being thoroughly ground up and unidentifiable. Reptiles and birds are okay, but people get weirded out about other species. Obviously, our customers who need items that aren't on display know what to ask for."

"You'll still be making my youth masque, won't you, dear? I have no talent for that particular magic," Natalie asks.

"I mean, yeah...but, it's an example, you know what I mean. Use common sense."

Nat goes behind the counter and stows her red purse beneath. "Do you really think that the high priestess of the Giles coven needs lessons in common sense from a whippersnapper like you?"

I stand my ground. I love Nat dearly, but if she gets on a roll, worse things than fetal pig could show up on display on the counter top. "You know what I mean." I glare. Her lips quirk beneath a glare of her own.

"I do. But I've been using magic since before your father was born. And coming into this shop for almost as long. So, unless you plan to stick name tags on us, go on with you. We've got it handled."

"Yes, dear, we're fine," Gillian adds. She waves a

limp hand at the door, shooing me away. "I'll make sure she doesn't turn any of the punters into toads."

Wow. I know when I've been dismissed. And Dash is expecting me. Plus, I want to stop by the diner and see how Tom is doing. I'm sure they can manage it if they don't end up in a duel with wands at ten paces and accidentally send the shop into an alternate universe or something.

The stray puppy—I think of him as Blackie now—is outside the door waiting for me, and I can't resist rubbing his belly when he rolls over all cute like that. The time just flies away while we play, and I end up running down the street with no time to stop in and see Tom at the diner like I said I would.

I'm sure Dash is just about to say something about my tardiness, but then he sees Blackie behind me and says instead, "I see you've brought your friend."

"Yeah, he's cute, isn't he? He keeps following me around."

"I think he'll make a fine pet for you. Jon and I adopted an older dog ourselves a couple of months ago. We simply felt compelled, and now we find her companionship enlightening."

He doesn't even mention me being late.

***

I want to get away on break to check how Gillian and Nat are doing in the shop—I'm sure they're doing fine, but if either of them has the ability, they could also be throwing lightning bolts at each other over a disagreement about where to put the herbal teas. They seemed fine when I left, but you never know when one of them might say something that rekindles bad feelings now that their rivalry for Robert's attentions culminated in Gillian walking away with the prize.

I wasn't around for most of it, being possessed by a demon-goddess and all, but Gillian filled me in. It apparently took Tom forever to catch on. I don't think he really wanted to think of Gillian as having moved on from him.

Nuts. I promised myself I wasn't going to think about Tom and Gillian like that. It's way in the past. Way, way in the past. There's absolutely no reason that I should be jealous.

Just as we're getting ready to close up the gallery, Greta Mason, who's some kind of bigwig on the city council, and her husband come in. Dash looks disappointed, like he doesn't want to stay, and I don't mind staying a little late. I give a quick call to Gilly, and she says they'll have no problem at all closing up without me. Which means the shop is still standing, at least.

I send Dash home and manage to sell Councilwoman Mason a nice modern bronze that Dash recently marked down. I know the artist, he's local out of Boston, and he's going to be so pleased.

Blackie walks me home. I forget to stop in the diner again, but by the time I'm back to the shop, there's no point in going back down the street to check in with Tom. I head upstairs to take a nap. I'm suddenly feeling exhausted.

***

I wake up when Tom's voice breaks into my dreams, "Cass! You brought that dog into our bed? I told, I...I mean, if you really want a pet, we could get a cat—the full-time kind, not the me kind."

I don't even remember him coming with me, but Blackie is definitely sleeping by my side. He's so warm where he snuggles against me.

"Sorry. I'll get him out of here. I must have been really tired. I don't know how he got in."

I don't think Tom believes me about that one. He's a fine one to talk, given what *he* recently left in the bed. My bed companion is a whole lot more savory.

Blackie whines and looks so sad when I set him out back, saying, "Look, you gotta go home. I know you must have a home, because you're well fed and looked after. So, go on."

He turns and trots down the alley.

"I thought you were going to stop by today," Tom says when I join him in the kitchen. He doesn't turn to me. He keeps rustling around in the fridge instead, but I hear the disappointment in his voice.

"I meant to. But then it got busy at the gallery—I sold that nice bronze, by the way. Remember, the one with the delicate birds around the base? The artist will be thrilled. We've had it so long that Dash has been making noise about sending it back unsold."

He must have looked at everything in the fridge at least twice by now. Finally, he asks, "How hungry are you? Is salad okay? I've been cooking all day, and I don't think I can face one more skillet. I wanted to bring home some of the stew I made for the daily special, but it got slurped up long before the dinner crowd. I think Giles is more than ready for a shift back to honest food."

I shrug. I'd really like to bring up that we still seem to be fighting, but I don't want to start it up again. With all of the changes with the diner and the shop, of course we're both stressed. I ask, "Will there be warm bacon dressing?" instead.

He smiles back at me over his shoulder. "I think I can manage that."

"I'm in for salad then. Can I do anything?"

"Set the table?"

I grab what we need and fill two wine glasses from the box in the fridge. Tom still thinks boxed wine is a crime against nature, but he doesn't actually refuse to drink it, so my handy box gets to keep its pride of place. I never said I was a connoisseur. That's Tom's job.

"So, anyway, about not stopping by...I got busy, and I walked home. Blackie must have followed me," I say, as I scoot by Tom in the small space. Usually being this close to him would set me tingling. But, nothing. No tingles.

He frowns as he sets the plates of salad down and goes back to the counter for the dressing. "You named it?"

"Him. I've rubbed his belly enough times to know he's a he. And yes, I named him."

"I can see I'm not going to win on this. That dog's moving in, isn't it?"

"I told you I wouldn't. I get it. I know why we can't have a dog. Truthfully, I've never even wanted a dog before. I was so excited when I met Granny and she had a cat. I love cats. Oh wait...that was you." I grimace and pick up a forkful of salad instead of continuing with that line of thought. One thing is for sure: I shouldn't have picked Tom if I wanted an uncomplicated relationship.

Still, it sucks that my choice of boyfriend prevents me from having a pet in my own house.

IT'S MY DAY in the shop since the gallery is closed on Fridays. Tom went to the diner hours ago, and neither of my new staff come in until later.

Minutes after I open up, Cinnamon wafts in smelling strongly of patchouli and cannabis, her caramel-colored skin set off by a white poet blouse over black slacks. I'm not really sure I want to see her. Blackie sits outside looking mournful about being shut out as she approaches me at the counter.

"Did you think any more about adding my readings to the shop's offerings?"

"I need to ask my staff about it now." I finish sorting tea into variety bags and arrange them in the sale basket. They look enticing tied up with their shiny ribbons. "Gillian and Nat are going to be managing the day to day operations of the shop, and

I'll need to find out if they think it will be disruptive to what they have planned."

She doesn't look very happy about that. "I see. But what do *you* think of it?"

"I think your reading was upsetting, and it made me think my boyfriend was doing the dirty on me when he wasn't."

"I have a gift, Cassie. I don't make things up. But the cards are open to interpretation. They can be tricksters. I'd be happy to do another reading for you."

I roll that around for a minute, and it rolls smoothly enough, without sharp edges. "Okay, sure." What can it hurt, right?

A small, tight smile pulls up the corners of her mouth. "That's appreciated."

I get the card table out, and she lays the deck on the table for me to shuffle and cut. She begins to lay out the cards like she did before, looks at them with a strange expression on her face, and then says, "This isn't possible!"

She gathers them up and makes me shuffle and cut again.

She lays them out and shakes her head back and forth violently. "No! It can't be."

I see it now. The cards are the same as the first time she read them for me. Every one in the same place.

I grab the cards back up and shuffle, shuffle,

shuffle, then cut again, and she lays them out. But it's the same.

"Are you manipulating them?" she asks, a look of suspicion in her eyes. "Using your magic?"

I shake my head. "No. Why would I do that?" I return the suspicious look. "Are you?"

She shakes her head slowly. She looks...well, she looks scared. I don't think she's faking it.

She says, "The cards haven't changed. Your past, your future. They remain as I said. You'll be deceived. You could lose everything you love."

I stand up abruptly. "Look, I don't think I need a big negatron with a mean streak giving readings in my shop. That would be bad for business."

She stands, scooping up the cards from the table noisily and stuffing them into her purse. "I wouldn't do another reading in this cursed place if you begged me. I'll find a place in Salem. Anywhere but here." She hurries out and down the street, but Blackie doesn't trail her this time.

Instead of following her, he darts across the street as she exits, and my heart judders painfully when I see the oncoming car rushing toward him. Blackie stops dead—I figure he's terrified by the whoosh as it approaches—but he stares at the driver like he's daring her, and she lands on the brakes hard, making the car bounce back on its springs when it stops several feet away from him.

He continues across the street unharmed.

Whew. The little guy just caught one lucky break.

***

Tom is on a high after a good day at the diner. I let him talk, nodding once in a while, but it doesn't really register. All I can think about is the reading that came out the same way every time. That came out awful. Betrayal by a loved one. A friend turning out not to be a friend. Losing everything. A year ago, I would have laughed about it, thinking that people who pay attention to things like tarot readings were silly. But a year ago, I didn't know I was a witch or have an enchanted boyfriend who shares his body with a cat.

We clean up the dishes, and he says he's taking Cat out hunting but promises he'll be back in time to meet Gillian and Robert at the gazebo for the last community concert of the year. It's bluegrass tonight, which I know nothing about, but Tom says it should be a good time.

He leaves his clothes, wallet, and the diner keys in a pile in the upstairs parlor and then Cat's out the window, ready to prowl.

That's my boyfriend. But is he "catting around" in more ways than one?

I'd bring it up, confront him again, but he'd just sweet talk me with the same old same old.

There's nothing going on Cass. I'd never hurt you like that, Cass. I love you, Cass.

I might as well have stayed with Dan.

Stayed with Dan? No way I just thought that! That would have been like the worst possible way to spend my life.

I have to stop thinking about that stupid tarot reading. But it's weighing me down big time. I mean, how weird was that? Both the ten of swords and the three of cups—upside down, too—over and over again. And Cinnamon's all pompous, "certain a friend will betray you" routine. How did she even manage it with me shuffling the cards each time?

I watched her hands, and she must be slick, because I couldn't see her doing anything unusual. Of course, it could be magic instead of sleight of hand. It would take a lot of skill to change the faces of the cards as she reveals them, but I'm learning that there isn't much in the natural world that's impossible if you know the right people. Or maybe it was an illusion she cast just on me and other people would see the cards differently?

That has to be it! An illusion would be a lot easier than changing the order of the cards in the deck or transforming the pictures on the cards.

I have one of Gillian's early grimoires, and I start leafing through to see if there's anything there that would let me duplicate the trick and figure out how she did it. I'm still scanning through it when there's a huge crash out in the street.

I hustle to the front window to see what's going on, and one of the big metal trash receptacles that line the sidewalks downtown is rolling around in the street in front of an older car that has a big dent in the fender.

The driver gets out and starts pulling the trash can back to the sidewalk. Wow. How would that get into the middle of the street in the first place? We don't usually get much vandalism in Giles, but every so often someone lets loose. My granny used to say it was the poltergeists who pushed the benches and trash cans over. Could be true for all I know. We might have a whole flock of them. It would take a lot of work to cut through the chains that keep those heavy steel can holders from being carted away, though.

My eyes are drawn to where there are a few others standing out on the street, local business owners and people on their way to the concert in the center of town, I suppose, taking in the same scene I am. A big crash like that is bound to draw just about everyone outside.

In front of the diner, Tom and Gillian are standing together looking at the scene of the accident. Down at the end of the street, Robert walks toward them, big smile on his face as he heads toward them from behind.

His smile makes me smile. Robert is one of the last of the good guys. I love seeing him so happy.

But what's happening? What's going on? No.

No!

Tom and Gillian turn to each other, lean in, and just like that, they're in each other's arms, their lips meeting, and they're grinding on each other, their hands grasping each other's hair in the passion of their kiss. He's wearing the clothes she keeps in a bin for him outside her garage, in case he's out prowling and wants to stop for a visit.

I guess I know why he had to cache some clothes there, now. He's got hiding places all over town these days, so I never thought a thing about it.

Robert stops dead in his tracks, as dead as I feel, his smile morphing into a twisted slash of pain. He turns abruptly and walks stiffly back toward his SUV.

Me? I can't watch a second longer. Not one second.

I rage through the house in a fury, slamming the windows shut and locking the doors. If Tom thinks he's ever getting back in here, he's crazy. I'm sure he'll think he's getting out of this one, too, but no way. No way in seven hells.

Tom Sanders is never going to get a chance to tell me another lie.

As I pad silently along, I smell dog all over downtown tonight. Man, that's nasty. I'll be giving the bright red downtown hydrants a wide berth to save any further insult to my sensitive nose.

I'll keep Cat away from that pup if it's hanging out at our place again or shows up at the concert, but I'm only doing it because I promised Cassie. I'd be plenty happy if it just disappeared. Even if Robert's wrong and the puppies are somehow related to Anat, he's right about one thing, and I know it: there's no reason to think she can hurt us any more. And those pups? Smelly, but harmless.

Cat jumps when a thundering crash echoes loudly through the alley, coming from the street. I sprint out front to see what's going on. Looks like it's just a fender bender in front of the bakery. Good. Nothing that can make trouble for Cass. Not even magic-induced.

And there's that pup again. It's right in the thick of things, watching from across the street.

And another one a little further along-and another near a couple who are having a face-sucking session smack dab in front of the diner. Man, a whole litter must be hanging around downtown tonight.

Wait a minute! The face-sucking woman is definitely Gillian, but that's sure not Robert she's hoovering. In fact, Robert is coming down the street toward them. No, he's turning now and walking away fast. He's got to be devasted: how could Gillian—sweet, kind, never-hurt-a-fly Gillian—do this to him? I have to go after him.

I jump off my fencepost and start down the street. And then...what the hell?

The guy she's with? It's me.

But I'm pretty sure *I'm* me. Or Cat's me. Or... What the hell?

I zoom toward the couple to find out what's going on. Robert is already backing around and heading out the other end of the street. I'm not going to catch him.

And then the couple disappears. Poof. Gone.

I look around, and there are more of the small black dogs sneaking around than I thought—I count five now. When I meet eyes with the one in front of the shop, its lips rise in a drooly doggy smile. Then it bolts around the side of the building through the narrow side yard.

I skim along after it. Cat can catch it, I'm sure. I need to get to the bottom of this and do it now. Robert needs to know that what he saw wasn't real. After losing his son this past summer, no matter what kind of a nightmare Kevin was, there's no way he can lose Gillian, too.

I round the back corner of the shop in time to see Cassie pick up the pup and close the door behind her. I dash for it to get inside before it closes—I have to protect her from that thing, but she slams it tight. I hear the dead bolt slide into place.

Her face twists up with tears and anger as she yells from behind the window, "Don't even try to get out of it this time, Tom. I saw what you did! Don't ever talk to me again."

She disappears, taking the smirking canine with her.

I move fast, shimmying up the tree to the second floor where there should be a window open for Cat to jump in from the branch, but the window is closed.

What do I do now?

I sit on the wide branch and fight to think rationally. Then the window opens and a pile of clothes and shoes comes flying out.

"And take your stuff. I don't want anything left to remind me of you. I believed you were different!"

I shimmy back down the tree and shift painfully

in the brisk night air. I shiver as I get dressed. At least she didn't cut the crotch out of my pants like she did to Dan's after she found him in bed with her best friend. That's something, isn't it?

I take inventory. I've got four pairs of jeans, seven shirts, two undershirts, a week's worth of jockey shorts, a pair of sandals, a pair of boots, a wallet with ten dollars in it, my cell phone, and a keyring that now contains only one key—the key to the diner.

That really is everything I own. Except the ring I haven't picked up yet from the jewelers. My throat tightens until I check the hidden compartment in my wallet. The receipt's still there. The receipt for my second most precious thing.

I never even got the chance to pick up the ring before it all went wrong. And my very most precious thing has just barred the doors and windows to keep me out, making the second most precious thing absolutely worthless.

***

I try to call Cass, but she's not answering. Same with Gillian. Same with Robert.

Goddess, what a mess. I should have known that me and Cassie working toward a future together, having the diner back, all of it, was too good to be true. I should have followed that dog the day it was lurking around us in the woods to kill her and the pups inside her belly. I should never have given her a chance to come at me again.

But it's too late now. Hindsight is 20/20. No use crying over spilled milk.

No matter how many cliches I throw at it, the truth is, I'm tired. I'm tired to my very soul of being locked into this battle with some death-denying goddess who chose me at random for her favors. So, I'm going to sleep on it. In the back of the diner here, on a pile of semi-clean towels and table cloths.

Tomorrow, I'll gird my loins, don my battle gear, and figure out a way to take that demon dog down for good.

I GET THROUGH to Gillian in the morning. She says, "I'm at the house. My house. I've been banished from Robert's."

Her voice catches, and I say, "I'm coming over. Just sit tight."

It takes me longer to get there on Tom feet than it would on Cat feet, but I have no interest in slipping into the clothes I have stowed in a box next to her garage. With the way things have been going for me, I'm sure a snap of me sans pants in Gilly's backyard would somehow end up on the front page of the local paper.

She sits in the middle of the living room floor, luggage and boxes piled around her. Polly is in his cage. He says, "Pretty Tom, pretty Tom, pretty Tom," over and over again until I pick his cage up and carry him upstairs where he can talk to himself.

I'm not in the mood for it today. I wish we'd never taught him my name.

I come back to the living room and give Gillian a hand up. She doesn't take it at first. Her eyes and nose are red. The pile of dirty tissues on the end table tell me she has been sitting here like this for a long time.

I get her into a chair and go to the kitchen to put the kettle on. She's British, so it never fails: life will feel more under control once she's got a cuppa in hand.

When I return with the hot tea, I ask, "What happened? I bet I know, but please me tell what you know about it."

Her face screws up into a tear-fighting knot before it smooths out again and she says, "Robert says he saw us—you and me—canoodling in public in front of the diner. He packed up my things and put them in the car and told me that if I didn't leave, he'd have the police escort me."

"That's bad. I can't imagine Robert being that angry."

"I was afraid for Polly. That stray that's been hanging around was strutting around like he owns the place, and he was really eyeing Polly up."

"Okay, and *now* I can imagine it." When I drop into one of Gillian's flowery, overstuffed arm chairs, I feel like a rag doll. My arms hit the chair's arms with a loud, empty clump.

"What do you mean?" she asks.

"Remember what happened when the Goddess tricked Anat into leaving Cassie?"

Gillian looks thoughtful for a moment. "That's right, she headed for the dog on the edge of the clearing."

"Exactly."

"But that puppy is too young, Tom. It can't be the dog from that night."

"No, but after Robert buried Kevin's ashes, do you remember when I went off into the woods?"

"Yes. We thought you had to see a man about a unicorn, so to speak."

"And I let you think that. Because I didn't want to make the day worse by telling you what I'd seen. But it was that dog. The one Anat took over. And she was pregnant. Robert knew, but I thought I'd nuetralized that threat."

"Are you saying that she's spawned an entire litter of demonic dogs? Don't be ridiculous. She couldn't pass her magic on to them."

"I think she has. I know she has. Robert described to you what he saw us doing together. Well, I saw it, and Cassie saw it, too. It was perfectly timed to make sure both of them would see. And who else would have an interest in ruining our lives but our old friend Anat? Who knows how long she's been waiting for just the right moment to twist the blade."

"Exactly what did you see?" she demands.

"Five little black dogs staring at the spot where

you and I stood together with our tongues stuck down each other's throats in something that was definitely not just a friendly gesture."

Her hand moves to cover her mouth as she starts to sob. Between tortured breaths, she says, "No wonder Robert was furious. I would have treated him the same if I'd seen him like that with someone else."

"You wouldn't have. You're kinder than that. And Robert wouldn't have treated you this way without a push. I mean, were you at the house when he got back?"

"Yes, I was. I was just finishing up packing a hamper for the concert before I went to meet him. Come to think of it…how could he think it was me he saw if he came straight home? That doesn't make sense. He should have known I couldn't have gotten back before him if he'd just seen me downtown."

"That's what I mean. He was being influenced. He's not thinking like himself, and if Anat Jr. has moved in, I don't think Robert's going to come to his senses unless we can get the beast away from him."

"Oh Goddess, Tom," she says quietly, her head still down in her hands. "Not again. I don't know if I have any fight left in me."

When she raises her head again several minutes later, we drink tea and stare at each other. Neither one of us seems to know what to say.

Finally, she sets her tea down. "You can't stay

here, Tom. Not if there's any chance Robert might regain his senses. I just don't want to chance it. Not given what he thinks he's seen."

I don't think it will make much difference since even if I'm not here, my arch-nemesis can make it look like I am, but I don't put up a fight. "I can sleep in the diner. Robert can't toss me out me since the paperwork for the lease is already done."

"No, that's not right. Plus, wouldn't the health department have something to say about it if they find out you're living there? No, I'm calling Nat."

***

Nat arrives to pick me up about half an hour later. She bustles in the door, making jokes, "It's about time Robert realized the better woman didn't win. What's his favorite wine, dear? Just so I get that right?" But she stops short when she sees the state Gillian is in. She's not always the most sensitive person in the room, but she's not out and out mean, either.

We fill her in on everything that's happened and although she doesn't express sympathy to either one of us, other than a hmmmm or two, she starts right in planning and plotting.

"Tom, did you see the older dog, the one that Anat took over? Or did you just see the pups?"

"No, I didn't see the adult dog. I just saw the five young ones—the one that followed Cassie, the one that must have followed Robert, and three others. I don't know where they all went. I was too busy tracking the one that went back to the shop."

"Well then, that's our first job. Find out where they went, and where their dam is holed up. Once we know that, we should be able to take them out. We don't have to worry about harming anyone like we did when Anat took Cassie. None of the people involved are possessed, so we can remove Anat's canine minions one by one and things should go back to normal."

"Will they?" I say. "Or will Cassie and Robert still believe that they saw what they saw? I can't see Cass forgiving me for murdering her new pet. And what's to stop Anat from grabbing another dog or cat or bird or cockroach?"

Nat harumphs. "I'll worry about demonic cockroaches when the threat surfaces. Until then, you can't just let this be simple?"

"Is it ever simple?"

"Could be. If the two of you weren't so obsessed about your love lives all the time."

Gillian rouses. "Nat, I've had enough. I know that you're hurt because Robert chose me over you, but we both care about you, and we tried to be careful with your feelings. You haven't made it easy. But if you don't want to help, then just go on and get out. Tom and I will manage on our own."

Nat turns to her, brings her hand to her chin, looking down at her from beneath half-closed lids, then raises a finger-tip and taps her pursed mouth for a moment.

Finally, she lifts the eyebrows that match her bobbed, platinum hair and says, "You have no idea how close you just came to being turned into a hamster. But..." She lowers her hand and starts digging in her ever-present red vinyl purse, "...fortunately for you, I know when it's time to stop fighting the current. What do you Brits say? 'Let's get stuck in?'"

***

I put my small store of possessions away in the dresser drawer Nat cleared for me in her guest room. They don't fill it completely. She might as well have cleared me out a shoe box. What I've got isn't much to show for a whole life. Without Cassie, it's nothing at all.

I call down the hall, "Nat, I'm going out. Don't close the bedroom window, please."

"Wouldn't think of it," she calls back.

It doesn't take Cat much time to be back up in the tree just outside the upstairs parlor above the shop. Yes, this is who I am now: an obsessed stalker trying to get a glimpse of the woman who has told me in no uncertain terms she never wants to see me again. But I'm not letting go. Not while I've still got one life left that I could be spending with her.

She's watching TV, her new pet lounging across

her lap, her fingers absently fondling a glass of wine on the end table. She doesn't look angry or broken-hearted. She just looks vacant.

Then that damn dog jumps up and starts yapping at me. Cassie gets up, walks to the window, expressionless, and closes the blinds. She doesn't even acknowledge me.

"SHUT UP! Shut up! Both of you. You're doing my head in!" Gillian screams.

That never happens. She must really be a mess. Our breakfast meeting had started out fine, all crullers and cooperation over the living room coffee table, but things went downhill fast.

Nat and I exchange a glance, and then we both fold our hands in our laps and wait for whatever's coming next.

She takes a deep breath. "All the two of you have done for the past half hour is quibble about who's going to spy on who, and who's going to be in charge of what. Neither one of you will compromise. You're like children. One of you has to be in charge. Decide who that is."

"Well, obviously, that's me," Nat says, rubbing up a little ball of dangerous-looking red magic at the tips of her fingers.

I stay calm. I don't need to start fighting with her again. Especially when she's in the mood to kill something. "Look, Nat. I get it. I don't have my own magic, and I'm definitely not a natural leader. But I'm the one who knows Anat the best. I understand her motivations. And that's going to help us more than magic. I need to step up, and you need to step aside."

"Well, flapping frog fritters!" She pauses and her eyes narrow. "When you say it that way, it obviously makes sense. But when this Anat character is out of the way for good, you don't challenge me again." She folds her arms across her chest and gives me a penetrating look.

I drag a finger across my own chest one way and then the other to make an X. "Cross my heart, Nat. I don't want anything to do with any of this. I'd be happy to never have known magic existed. But that bitch has interfered between me and Cassie for the last time."

"You do exude a certain leadership quality—or maybe it's just sex appeal—when you talk that way. So, I'll step back. Be your right hand man, so to speak. It's not like Gillian's going to be up to it."

We both look to Gilly. She gives a shrug and a sad smile. "Having Robert look at me that way, like I was filth, it's taken all the fight out of me."

I stand and walk to her, give her a supportive hug. "Just for a little while, I bet. And I know if I need you, you won't let me down. So, no more fighting for us. Time to get back to what really matters."

They both nod their heads in agreement.

"Look, if you can't plan the battle, can you make tea for the planners?" I ask. Gillian heads toward the kitchen, so I guess she can.

I lean back in one of the flowery, overstuffed arm chairs and cross my ankle over my knee, one elbow on the arm of the chair, stroking my chin.

"Tom! Don't let Gillian see that," Nat says, giving me a fierce look.

"What? Oh…geez." I realize I'm unconsciously mirroring one of Robert's contemplative moves. Great. Now I have to worry I'll set her off because I've picked up some of my friend's mannerisms. I was always a natural mimic, even as a kid. I don't need it getting me in trouble now.

I lean forward again, elbows resting on my thighs, my feet firmly on the floor at a masculine distance from each other. Yes, that's more like me.

"Okay, Nat. What I need from you is information on what Cassie is doing on a daily basis. Watch her every move during the day at the shop if you're working together and try to find out what she's doing when she's not there."

"Why can't I just walk in, magic blazing, and incinerate the beastie that's causing the problem?"

"Because we don't know what effect that would have on Cassie. I'm not risking hurting her. And it won't help us locate Anat. So just don't go off half cocked." I stare her down. She glares back, and then she nods, accepting the terms. I continue, "And...Gilly's not going to like this part..."

"What part am I not going to like?" Gilly asks as she comes back into the room with a tray of tea biscuits.

"I want Nat to pretend that she's moving in on Robert now that you're out of the way. It would seem natural to Robert that she would, and he's not completely opposed to her that way, right?"

She closes her eyes for a moment, and the corners of her mouth turn down almost imperceptibly.

I realize my mistake. "I'm sorry, no, that's a terrible idea."

"Yes, a truly terrible idea," Nat agrees. "What would I want with someone else's leftovers? There's no way I could pull it off. No one would believe it for a minute."

That's not true, of course. Everyone would believe it, and I'm sure Nat knows that.

Gilly knows, and she looks grateful. "Thank you."

"What for?"

"For taking my feelings seriously. I know how difficult it is for you to stop joking around, and I appreciate it."

"Yes. That's fine." Nat turns back to me abruptly, expressionless. She asks, "And while I'm risking life and limb spying on people who are being controlled by our neighborhood canine goddess, what will you be doing?"

"I'm going into deep cover. I'll be making the rounds as Cat. No one pays attention to a cat. And with the number of black cats in this town, even the people who know about me are unlikely to suspect me. My anonymity was a big part of how Eunice kept herself in power all those years. Now it's time to put everything I learned to better use. I'll be tracking the other dogs and trying to find out where dear old mom is hiding out."

"It sounds like a plan. Any more details?" She shoves a cup at Gillian, not even looking at her. "More tea."

I really wish Robert was here. He's always a stabilizing force between these two. So now I know what our first step has to be: we need him to complete our rebellion. And there's no reason we can't move right now.

***

"Just stop worrying, Tom. I've got your back," Nat hisses in my ear where we hide behind the bushes at City Hall. There's not a lot of traffic in and out, and the police force is mostly patrolling, but I'm still not convinced we're going to have the easy time of it Nat thinks we will. It's bad enough Robert is bringing his own pet to work—a quick peek in his office windows confirmed that—but a stray cat roaming the municipal offices will definitely raise some eyebrows.

"Just go on. I'll keep an eye out. And Gillian has the car running. We'll get the dog away and bring Robert back to his senses, I'm sure of it."

I creep along beneath the bushes until I'm near the door. Cat fixes his eyes on the enticing, transparent violet wave of the magic Natalie uses as it hits the door and opens it enough for Cat to slide through. He's worried about our tail and puts an extra bit of rocket into his glide, and we're all the way through and heading down the hall toward Robert's office in the back of the building before I can make sure the door is being kept open for our retreat.

This place has that just-painted, just-bleached institutional smell to it that marks so many government buildings. I'd prefer a little whiff of dirt. It would feel less like things are being covered up. Then again, in a town like Giles, there's plenty to cover. Robert has had his hands full with a town full of eccentric witches for a long time.

I keep to the wall, peering through each open door before I pass. I smell the pup before I can see it. I stick my head out around the door frame and it spots me immediately.

I expect it to growl or paw at Robert's leg. I'd assumed I'd have to attack to actually draw it away, but things turn out better than I'd hoped. I don't need to do much to get its attention. I know it must be connected to Anat somehow, but it's clearly still mostly dog. When it sees a cat, it can't help but give chase.

I tear off in the other direction, and I hear it panting behind me, trying to catch up. Not going to happen. Cat can really cover the ground, at least for short distances.

I dart out through the door and hear the dog pushing through behind me with a little yelp.

This is working. I'm drawing it away. If I can get it out of whatever range it needs to influence Robert, I may be able to break its hold.

But I also hear Robert calling it back.

Rover? He named it Rover? Man, the guy really needs saving.

Nat's waiting in the bushes to snatch up the pup in a bag she prepared especially to dampen any influence coming from the miserable creature. I slide gracefully in next to her after my run to share her hiding place. I turn back quickly to watch the pup heading toward us from between the leaves. But before it even makes if off the building's steps, a big cop hustles toward the entrance from the parking lot and scoops the pup up as it tries to skitter by him with its nails clacking against the concrete.

"Oh no, you don't. I don't think the mayor will be happy if you end up splat under the wheels of a passing car. Let's get you back inside."

He heads for the door, which Natalie had allowed to close after the pup got through, and Robert opens it, then gives a stiff smile when he sees the pup being returned.

He takes it from the cop without a word and heads back in. No thank you from Mr. Congeniality? How can these people not know the man's not himself?

Cat creeps back under the bushes and brushes against Nat's legs. He's not the least bit bothered. He had a victory. He escaped his pursuer. But me? I'm far from celebratory. That's one step in my plan down the tubes already, and it may also have tipped Anat off that I'm on to her.

***

I shift awkwardly in the back of Gilly's small economy car and get dressed while the ladies keep their eyes to the front. Even Natalie, who is all business now as she fills Gillian in.

"If the officer hadn't come around the side of the building when he did, this would be sorted. We'd have the pup away, and you'd be back in your lover's arms."

"So, that's it. We can't try again?"

"It's up to Tom. But I think we'll be expected next time, don't you? There appears to be an intelligence working behind all of this. If it were me, I wouldn't let something that was almost successful play out again under my watch." Natalie flings her black, fringed scarf around her neck forcefully. "We should assume we're not getting away with something similar again."

I've gotten myself straightened out now and need to gather some intelligence of my own. "Do you think it saw you, Nat?"

She turns to look at me over her shoulder. "I don't think it did. But that doesn't mean I'm in the clear."

Gillian nods her head as she pulls cautiously out of our parking spot a block from City Hall. "Natalie, I'll drop you at the shop. No point you being late to work. Tom, you'll need to stay down. I don't want us being seen together. I'm going back to talk to Robert after I drop Nat and stop you off at her house."

"No, you're not going to see Robert!" I tell her.

"I am."

I'd say I forbid it, but that would have them both rolling on the floor laughing—a dangerous deal when one of them is driving the car. I mean, I like women who know their own minds, but just once I'd like to have one of the women in my life follow instructions without giving me lip. Particularly when what I just said makes sense.

"Gillian, there's nothing you can say to him right now, and who knows how much influence Anat has over him? You really can't do this," I say, frustrated.

"I agree, dear. He's unpredictable right now. Not our calm Robert. You would be taking a big risk for no real gain," Natalie says, lending unexpected support.

Gillian's voice is low and quiet when she responds. "I just want to see him. Make sure he's all right." Then she barks out a command. "Down, Tom! There's a car approaching, and we're nearly there."

I don't have much choice, and it's hard to argue when my six foot tall body is crammed into the foot well. Not what you'd call a position of power.

After she lets Nat out and we're heading back to her place, I make my case from my cramped space behind the passenger side seat. "Don't you think I'd be waiting for Cassie every morning when she leaves the shop if I thought there was any chance she could be talked 'round? But I'm not. Because it would be wasted energy, and it would be risky, just like Nat said. And you're too smart to go against both me and Nat. I mean, how often do we actually agree on something?"

"You sent Nat off to keep a close eye on Cassie. That isn't risky?"

"You aren't Nat. She'll do anything it takes to protect herself, and you know it. Could you say the same thing about yourself?" I hate being stuck back here where I can't see her when she talks.

Gilly is quiet for a moment, then her voice floats to me over the seat back, "Anything? No. Not quote, unquote, *anything*."

"Exactly. And that's why I'd worry about you, but I'm not worried about her."

"Fine. But I need to be in this. I was wrong. I've found my fight again. Give me something I can do."

I wriggle my backside restlessly to bring back circulation, hoping the ride ends soon. Maybe the lack of blood in my butt has given an extra splash to my brain, because I come up with what seems like a pretty good idea that may even be safe. I say, "I've got a way you can see Robert without putting yourself at risk. How about you and I attend the next city council meeting? Aren't they every Tuesday?"

Although she can't turn back to me as she maneuvers the car around a turn, I hear the smile in her voice. "They are. And I've been meaning to get more involved with city politics."

As soon as I open the shop door, Nat breezes in wearing a fitted black pantsuit with black knee-high boots, her hair covered by a red chiffon scarf like some old-time movie star. She greets me with, "Morning, Cass. I'm here for another day of slaving away to serve the magical needs of the Giles community."

I walk outside to make sure Gillian isn't coming, too. I was sure it was Gillian's car I saw pulling up. I sent her a text yesterday morning to let her know her services are no longer needed, and that I had better never see her in the store again, either. But she's always interfering in my business, so I'm not convinced she'll stay away.

She's not outside, though. I make certain of that as I take a good long look one way and then another, standing on the sidewalk before I walk back inside.

"Heard from Gillian?" I ask as Nat hangs her jacket on a peg behind the counter, folds her scarf and stuffs it into a jacket pocket, and starts tidying what I thought was an already tidy counter.

"I did, dear. In fact, she dropped me off. But she let me know I'd have to find my own ride from now on. It was the most confusing thing." She bends down to chuck Blackie under the chin when he gets out of his basket and goes to greet her. "She said that she wouldn't be able to work in the shop any more and that was that. End of the conversation. Is there more to this story? Have you two fallen out?"

"I don't want to talk about it, Nat."

She gives me a you've-got-me-curious-now look, but I just walk into the back and grab my things, calling over my shoulder, "Come on, Blackie. It's time to go to work."

I need to get to the gallery. At least there won't be kisses making me late anymore.

I walk briskly down the street, my faithful Blackie capering at my heels. I'm glad to be leaving the shop behind, although I'm not thrilled that Natalie is looking after it. She'll be poking her nose into everything.

Hmmm...I wonder if a wart growing on the end of it would remind her to keep it out of things that don't concern her? I know how to remove one now. I wonder if I could reverse the spell to make one appear?

***

I lower the hatch in the Gallery's back room and make sure the oriental carpet on top looks natural after Dash disappears down the stairs where he's been spending his lunch hour lately. I ducked out for a quick play break with Blackie and feel refreshed, ready to face the lunch hour art-gazers.

He'll be back up soon, but until then, the last thing my kindly boss needs is for his secret place to be discovered. It hides the town's most precious secret, and it's too early for it to be revealed. Even I don't even know what it is, but I feel safe when I'm at the gallery in a way that I don't when I'm at home. I know that adjustments have to be made in Giles, and I feel sure that I'll be an important part of them.

When I'm satisfied that the hiding place is secure, I move to the curtain that covers the entryway into the gallery and brush it aside to discover our security has been breached.

It's that busybody, Natalie. I can't imagine why I ever liked her.

"Nat, we're closed for lunch. How did you get in? That door was locked. And why aren't you at the shop?"

She looks taken aback when I confront her, but I don't buy it. She's cagey. One to watch.

"It wasn't, dear. I walked right in. And I get a lunch hour, too, don't I? The "Out to Lunch" sign is up. I'd like to talk to Dash about the possibility of selling a few of my recent paintings. I've been prolific lately, and I certainly don't have room to store them. He's been able to move them in the past."

"He's not here."

"Oh. My mistake." She looks out the front display window and inclines her head toward Dash's cute but ridiculously tiny, yellow vintage sports car. "I felt sure that if his car was here, he'd be here. I don't think he even lets Jon drive the MG. Strange that he would run off without it."

"He's doing errands downtown. It would be silly to drive."

"Oh? Where exactly? Maybe I could catch up with him."

"I don't know, Nat. You need to leave. I want to go to lunch myself."

I can tell she hears the same slight scuffling I do from the back now by the "gotcha" expression on her face. "Are you sure he's not here?"

She starts for the curtain, but I head her off.

"I'm sure."

And then Dash pushes the curtain aside and nearly runs smack into her.

She smiles. "Dash, what a surprise! I was wondering if you'd be willing to take a few of my pieces this winter? I heard you're going to be working more closely with the local artists again."

He pushes her aside. "I don't have time for this. We're closed." He urges her toward the door with a hand on her back.

Blackie and Flower, Blackie's litter mate, follow behind him. Jon must have stayed downstairs.

Natalie glances down to the dogs, then turns her eyes back to Dash. "Fine. I'll check with one of the galleries in Salem. They always do better for me money-wise anyway. I just thought I'd give a local business the opportunity first."

Flower jumps up on the leg of Natalie's black pantsuit before she turns. Her tail wags happily, but instead of a pat, she gets a shove and a muttered, "Great pandering pentacles! What's the world coming to when everyone in town has to keep pets in their shops? What's next? Polly in the diner?"

Flower really wants her attention, but Natalie avoids looking at her. Then she's out the door with that nose she sticks into everything totally out of joint.

***

"Come on, girl. That's right..." Flower bounds into my arms. Dash smiles, approving. Blackie looks like he's jealous, but he won't be for long. Little

Flower isn't for me. I wish she was, but no, there are other plans and plans must be followed. Flower is about to have a new owner.

Blackie follows at my heels as I walk to the Magical Shop with Flower licking my face and wagging her tail the whole way. I'm sure she won't be as pleased with her new mistress. Who could be? I can't imagine Natalie being really kind to anyone or anything, not even a sweet little puppy. But that's who Dash says she's for, so there's nothing I can do.

The "Out to Lunch" sign is still on the door, which is exactly what I wanted. I know the perfect spot for Flower to conceal herself until the old witch returns. I set Flower down while I unlock the door. Both she and Blackie sit there looking serious, staring up at the lock as I slide the key in. As soon as it swings open, they both dart inside. So cute. Maybe I can have both of them once Natalie is no longer needed.

I step behind the counter and open the wooden cask where we keep the purification power. It's a popular item because most spells do better if you perform a cleansing first. There are a lot of spells cast in Giles. We sell it in bulk.

Yes, it's perfect. With the powder lifted out in its inner plastic bag and stored away until the barrel is free again, and plenty of air coming in from the finger holes we use to raise the lid, Flower will be comfortable while she waits. Nat will have to open the barrel when she starts the afternoon stocking and sees the bags of the stuff we keep on the counter have all been sold. When she does, she'll be looking right into Flower's eyes. And what amazing eyes she has.

I make my way back down the street with Blackie trailing, the last three bags of purification powder stuffed in the bottom of my purse.

***

Natalie's standing behind the counter when I return to the shop at dusk. I can't tell right away if she's met Flower or not. Then Flower struts around the edge of the counter. Her tail wags for a job well done.

"How were things in the afternoon?" I ask.

"Better than I would have expected, dear. I got such a delightful surprise when I started the restocking."

"There's a council meeting tonight that we should attend," I say.

Her eyes flick up for a second as if she's remembering something, and then she says, "Yes. But I'll have to change my plans. I need to make a call."

She doesn't move off for privacy. Why should there be secrets between us? We belong to the same tribe now.

"Gillian? I won't be at dinner tonight. I've made

other plans." She listens for a moment. "No...not tomorrow, either. I expect to be busy. Too busy for your silly heartache over Robert, I'm afraid."

I smile. She's done well. "I'll make us dinner before we go."

CAT IS TRYING to convince me its time to find a warm spot to take a nap, and I'm nearly ready to give in. I feel like I've peered in at every window in town. But all my sneaky-peeping has gotten me is yelled at, and, in one notable instance, beaned with a shoe. An older, classic wingtip. A nice one. I thought about setting up a good howl and trying for the other one, but how would I get them back to Nat's? It's not like Cat's got pockets built into his fur coat.

It starts spitting small seeds of cold rain, and I dart under a car to get out of the wet. Cat is perfectly willing to sneak around and poke into things that don't concern him, but when it involves getting soaked he stops being cooperative. I'm not going to be able to convince him to play along again until it lets up a little, so I let him go to ground. But I stay alert for the sound of someone approaching. No nap possible here. The last thing I need is to blow my last life under the wheels of somebody's Dodge because I didn't stay alert for an approaching driver.

Then, whoa! I've lucked out.

A small black form pads along across the wet, gray sidewalk, following a pair of sensible low heels. I know those rundown heels. They belong to Eunice's sycophant Zelda. Well, of course she'd be in on this. Wherever Eunice went, she was never far behind. And...wait for it...yes, the daughter is cruising along in her wake in stilettos. Those two were always in the thick of it when Eunice ran the town. And they're obviously still in the thick of it.

So, they've got one pup. That's three accounted for. Where are the final two?

I force cat to stick his head out into the rain for a better look around, but the street is empty now. Most of the shops are closed. The only thing with lights on is the art gallery. Cat shakes his head, annoyed, to sluff off the tiny drops that slide down his ears.

If I had my own heart right now instead of Cat's small, unemotional one, it would skip a beat as Cass walks out of the gallery with that dog, Blackie, behind her. They're followed by Dash, Jon, and another black pup.

Good. Four down. I've only got to find one

more. Or, at least just one more that I know about. But what would Anat want with Dash? He and Jon aren't even magical practitioners. They're just guys.

I don't like this one bit. Cassie, Dash, Zelda, Robert—what do they have in common? I understand Anat targeting the coven members. But where does Dash come into this?

I'm not going to get any answers tonight. Dash walks down the street to his canary yellow toy car, and Cassie walks toward the shop. She doesn't seem to notice the rain. Normally, she'd be sticking her hands in her armpits and complaining about the cold and hustling along to keep warm. But she's moving slowly now, head erect. She looks like a zombie.

I've got to get her away from that dog.

***

I scramble up the tree next to the house, hoping Cass has opened the window or at least pulled up the blinds. The lights are on inside, and the TV is blaring, but the blinds are still drawn, leaving me with nothing but a rectangular spot of light in the gray dusk.

I sit patiently, staring the blinds down while getting a lick in here and there to keep my fur gleaming. It's stable enough on this wide branch and I'm starting to get bored, so I let Cat go on a grooming binge. He's got a back leg stretched out in the air for balance, claws extended, while he sits doubled over to work at the inside base of his tail.

A black muzzle pushes up the blinds at the bottom and a set of black paws appears on the inside ledge. Then, a small head appears. Cat is instantly on his feet, ready for a showdown. He bristles.

Its eyes are just big, brown, puppy eyes at first. Then they glow faintly red.

And in my heart, I know that mama demon knows I'm here. I can't stay here and wait around for her to come barking up this tree. Before I have time to turn and shimmy down to the ground, the blinds pull up and Cassie and Natalie are both looking out at me, the same shared, blank, look in their eyes. Another pup jumps up next to the first one.

Number five. All present and accounted for.

I scramble down and take off for Nat's. It's pretty clear she's no longer an asset, and I need to get my stuff out of there before she keeps me from getting to it. I don't care about my clothes, but I need my wallet. It contains the receipt: I'm not giving up on that ring.

And I'm not giving up on Cassie.

This is just another pothole in the road to happiness. A pothole. Not a sinkhole. Not a yawning chasm.

Pothole.

The rain starts again. The droplets have turned

to tiny ice cubes now. They stick to Cat's coat and leave icy patches on the sidewalk and the road.

But I'm not stopping, and Cat stops protesting about how hard I'm pushing him when I flash him the memory of what happened the first time we went up against the creature with the glowing red eyes.

Neither one of us has forgotten the snap, the end of pain, the blackness.

LOCAL COUNCIL MEETINGS aren't usually my thing. In fact, I've never gone to one before, because my Granny never liked them, and I liked what Granny liked. But I'm enjoying this one. Natalie is silent, which never happens, and Blackie is sitting quietly at my feet. Such a good dog.

Robert stands behind the council table in front of the group of townspeople who've come to discuss the festival. I expect it's a larger group than usual—that horrid Gillian told me once that the city council usually talks to itself at the public hearings. She's here with Tom. No surprise there.

Tom better watch his woman, though. Because she doesn't seem to be able to keep her eyes off Robert.

No one is much interested in the town governance as long as they can go about their business without interference. Robert's seen to it that what they expect is what happens. But many residents make good money at the Witching Faire—I remember how much Granny looked forward to her receipts that day.

Robert looks down at a sheet of paper and then says, "Next on the agenda—and this is really what we're all here for, I believe—let's pull out all the stops at this year's Faire. The event is now a shadow of what it was in Giles's heyday. I remember when I was a boy, every resident turned out. I want to see that happen again."

There's some clapping and a couple of here-here's. Then I realize that's Natalie and I. We're enthusiastic supporters of the plan. The minute Robert says it, it just sounds right.

"What I'd like from you, since you all know your neighbors so well, are some ideas about what would bring everyone downtown for the event."

People raise their hands to be recognized at first, but it soon becomes unruly with people just shouting out. The ideas come thick and fast.

"Give away something everyone will want," says one.

"A nice frozen turkey just before Thanksgiving would go over well."

"Better yet, how about a chance to win a trip? A winter getaway to someplace warm!"

"I say just give 'em money to spend. In fact, gimme mine right now. I promise I'll be there." Scattered laughter follows.

Nat stands up. "I don't think any of that is big enough to get everyone in town out for the day. But what about raffling off the old Stanford mansion? Didn't you say earlier that no one knows what to do about it now that it's been left to the city, and the upkeep is costing a fortune? I know they say the old place is haunted, but I'd bet the residents of Giles would be thrilled to get a chance at winning the grand old place. I know I would. This could be a much better use for it than turning it into a museum no one wants or letting it decay into an eyesore."

Robert smiles and looks around at the other counsel members. "That's a fine plan, Nat. Very fine, indeed. The city gets rid of its white elephant, and someone who isn't afraid of a few ghosts gets a fine home or a chance to fix it up and sell it on at a profit, one of the two." The other council members' heads nod in agreement.

Robert bangs his gavel. "It's decided. The Stanford mansion is up for grabs to any resident who attends the fair, fills out a raffle ticket, and stays for the drawing. I can't see anyone staying home for this one."

Tom looks at me as people start to gather in small groups before filtering out. I turn away to find my litter mates and we gather in our own group around Robert. He glad-hands his cronies and townspeople alike, then, when they're all gone, he turns to us and smiles. I don't think he even noticed our exes were here.

"That worked like a charm. Now, let's talk about the real event."

I walk over to close the door and then return to the small circle of witches.

I TWIST MY HEAD back over my shoulder to see how things look in the mirror from back there, and I have to say I'm pleased. My costume for the Witching Faire clings in all the right places. I went through one of the trunks of Eunice's old clothes I'd put aside and found an elegant black dress from her youth, fitted from the shoulder all the way to the ground, with a wide slit at the knee running down the left side so that I can still walk comfortably.

With a black witch's hat and a wooden wand from the more touristy items in the shop, I'm definitely in the spirit. And Blackie's matching hat, rakishly affixed at an angle, is adorable. I admire us both in the mirror for a long while. It takes my phone ringing to bring me back to myself. Goodness. Mesmerized by my own appearance.

Well, I do look hot.

But no time to linger. It's time to open the shop. I shed my costume and fold it neatly, then stack it on the bed with Blackie's hat on top.

I open the shop, get Nat to work, and survey my domain. Everything seems to be in order when my back pocket buzzes.

I check my phone. It's Dan calling. I've been ignoring his calls for a long time now, but...well, why don't I speak to him? We had a lot of fun until that horrid ex-friend of mine seduced him. He would never have behaved that way on his own, I'm sure.

Blackie looks straight at me with an encouraging expression. Yes, I'm sure that's right. I haven't given Dan a fair shake. For the first time in months, I swipe right to pick up the call.

"Hi Dan."

"Cass? I'm so glad you answered. I've been going crazy with us apart. I know it looked bad the last time I saw you...."

"Yes, it did, but..." I realize I don't know what I want to say to him. Where the hurt used to be there's just a hole. Why was I ever angry in the first place? "Why don't you come over some time?" I say.

Where did that come from? Blackie worries at the hem of my jeans playfully. Oh, who cares, right? All I can think about right now is Dan's smile, his close-cropped blonde hair, and great abs. So unlike Tom with his long, messy hair and skinny legs.

It's funny, I never thought of his legs as skinny

before. I mean, he's lean, but I always thought he was fit. See? Falling out of love is easy once you can see a man's flaws. And how could a dog person possibly love a cat person? It just couldn't happen.

In fact, I'm beginning to think all of that Tom business was just infatuation.

Dan? Now, Dan has a lot to offer.

I'VE BEEN PROWLING around downtown since early morning, and Cat is starting to protest. He wants to slip into the alleys and backyards for a hunt, but I need him to stay vigilant.

Gillian has her car parked at the end of the street where she can see the action. Our plan to break Cassie free of Anat's influence isn't brilliant, but its the best we've got. Basically, it's the same thing that failed with Robert: I'll try to lure the dog away.

From my hiding place in the shadows in the alley across from the shop, I have a front row seat to watch Cassie finishing her opening routine for the day through the big front display windows. The black pup she's adopted sits at her feet.

Then Nat comes out from the back, carrying a stack of boxes. She unpacks them quickly and arrays their contents on an empty shelf and goes into the back again. She's dressed in the same clothes she was wearing yesterday except for a pair of Cassie's comfy slippers. Bunny slippers. Cute on Cassie. Frightening on Nat.

She's been at the shop all night? Great. Seems like Anat is closing ranks, keeping her minions close together.

It's torture waiting for the shop to open, but Cassie unlocks the front door soon enough. My target, the small black beast that accompanies her, frolics at her heels.

The first customer arrives, and I slip in with her, hiding behind her legs the best I can and then slipping around to the back of a set of shelves.

Nat hasn't reappeared, but Cassie is behind the counter, talking on the phone. I strain to catch what she's saying.

"I know. I've missed you, too."

Who is she talking to? I poke my head out from behind the shelves as far as I dare and point my ever-so-sensitive furry sound scoopers right at her.

"Yes, I would. I'd like to see you, Dan...why not tonight? Mmmmmm...oh, I remember...."

My world shatters: I scrunch low, pulling in further from the world, my traitor ears pulled back now, low to my head. I don't want to hear any more.

Then, from around the far side of the counter, Cassie's demon dog comes into view, teeth bared.

Man, did he pick the wrong time to mess with me.

Cat's hackles rise to answer the dog's ridiculous, tiny growl, and the fleshy sheath around his claws retract. Come and get us if you dare, midget monster mutt. We're ready for action.

I take a quick glance over my shoulder to the door for my way out—this needs to go to plan now. No, I'm trapped in here until that door opens again. My only immediate option is to go skyward to safety. Without a hitch, I'm two shelves up on the narrow end cap, and the pup can leap uselessly in my general direction as much as it wants, but it's not getting to me.

Cassie can, though, once she gets to an angle where she can spot me. She walks out from behind the counter, coming to see what's got her demon dog in such a frenzy. I pull in small. I don't want her to catch a glimpse of my tail and hurry it up.

The shop bell signals someone's exit or entry just in time. I launch myself toward the door and fly over the dog's head, landing right in front of the opening and dash outside before the incoming customer has time to let go of the handle.

Is the pup even behind me? If it didn't chase me, the plan is already sunk. I can't stop to look. And then there's a yap a few feet behind that tells me it made it out of the shop, too.

Cassie's voice rings out above the yelping. "Damn you, Tom! Stay out of my life!"

This time, I need to take care of business. No

more Mr. Nice Guy.

First option is to run the beast into traffic. But no, nothing coming from either direction. I bolt across the street with the pup in hot pursuit, but how far will it follow me? Will it get far enough away from Cassie that I can face it down and take it out by shifting and punching its lights out with big, man fists?

Wait, there…that's what I need.

I head for the alley across the street, where the thudding and thunking of items landing in the hopper signals that the weekly trash pick up is currently in progress down the cross alley behind. If I can maneuver this right…

I dart across the street and through the alley, the damned dog following close, yapping all the way. I could outpace it if I want, but its stupid barking lets me know exactly how close it is so I can keep its attention without getting nipped.

I hope Gillian doesn't miss her cue. But there's no time to worry about that. I've get hell on my heels.

I veer to the right at the end of the alley with the whining sound of the garbage truck hydraulics keening in my ears from the left. Perfect. A set of stairs up to the small loading dock at the back door of the bakery is directly in front of me, and its dumpster is on the other side. Cat's prowled here thousands of times. He knows the lay of the land. I rush up the steps and hope I'm still being followed.

I take my leap of faith.

Cat sails out across the top of the half-empty open dumpster from the end of the stair landing and hits the other side with his paws curled around the hard metal. Nothing to grab onto. But I can't fall into the thing. He hooks his paws around the lip and gives a mighty pull, his back claws scritching frantically at the unyielding metal beneath them.

His strong back legs push us up and outward as he works them against the side of the bin, pulling upward with his cupped paws. We're out the other side with one last leap onto the concrete pad below.

I turn, hackles still raised, ready to bolt.

The pup isn't so lucky. He doesn't have nifty cat paws to pull himself out of the mess he's jumped into.

His useless yapping goes unheard in the squealing of the hydraulics as the sanitation truck slides its hooks in and skewers the dumpster on its forks, ready to raise it. Soon, it'll be dumped and crushed. I say good riddance to bad rubbish.

Oh hell. No way.

Not when victory is this close.

The pup comes floating out of the hopper before the forks turn it for emptying. Behind him, Nat's standing on the loading dock I vacated such a short time ago, her right hand stretched out toward it, beckoning. An identical black puppy with a red bow affixed over its right ear slobbers at her ankles.

Our eyes meet. Hers are blank and Nat-less.

I'm no coward, but I'm no match for her powers, either. She's sorcery on steroids. Even Gillian would think twice about taking her on unless she had no other choice.

I grab my chance to run while she's still occupied. Here's hoping she stays focused on saving the dog and doesn't shift her magical attention to a small, swift cat with only one life left tearing away from her down the alley.

***

I make a dash for the waiting car which is right where we planned it would be. I jump in through the open back window and judder through the shift. My morphing brain registers that Cassie isn't in the car: another part of the plot gone wrong. I start to speak even before I've finished my transformation. Nothing could be more urgent.

"Natalie. She saved it," I force out. But it sounds more like a Cat's yowl than human speech. A tortured "Yaaah gaaah heaow."

Gillian looks back at me across her shoulder with wide eyes, her mouth open in a surprised gasp. I rushed up on her so quickly and silently I doubt she even knew I was there until my limbs started slamming against the seats as I transformed. "By the Goddess, Tom! You scared the life out of me."

"I failed. Natalie rescued it. Did you hear me?"

I grab the waiting pair of sweatpants off the

back seat and cover myself.

"Rescued the puppy?"

"Yes. I nearly lured Blackie away from Cassie, but Nat managed to save him at the last minute. Take off! Get us out of here!" The tires squeal as Gillian revs the engine and peels out of the parking space. "I'd really hoped she was just playing along. Spying. It's bad enough Anat has Robert, having someone as powerful as Natalie on the side of the enemy…"

"No. No. It doesn't really bear thinking about," she replies as she stops briefly at the cross street to look both ways. "But I've got a surprise for you that should lighten your mood. Let's get home and see if there's a silver lining in this cloud."

***

Gillian pops open the trunk and there Cassie is, trussed up and gagged.

I know I broadcast my feeling of horror to Gillian as I dart a look sideways at her. She doesn't look like some deranged psycho. She still looks like the same pleasant, pudgy, not-at-all-Norman-Bates Gillian I've always known. But there's no way Cassie deserved this. She's not making any noise. And she's not moving.

What did Gilly do?

Her reassuring hand comes down softly on my shoulder. "Tom, I know it looks bad, but it's not like she was going to come willingly. I was barely able to overpower her with my magic; if I hadn't taken her by surprise when you lured her canine companion away and Natalie followed the both of you, she would have been too strong for me. I had to immobilize her."

I start to untie her. Gillian's hand moves swiftly from my shoulder to my wrist to stop me.

"No, let me wake her up first, and we'll see if she's going to continue to fight us. She's becoming a powerful witch, Tom. If she doesn't want to be here, she can give us a lot of trouble."

I know she's telling the truth. But this is Cass, my Cass, and I can't stand seeing her this way much longer.

Gillian passes her hands over Cassie's eyes, and they open. She looks terrified, then she looks from Gillian to me, her eyes pleading, and a tear forms and slides down one cheek.

I can't wait. And we're miles away from her demonic pet now. Everything I've seen tells me they have limited range and have to be able to make visual or physical contact to keep the bond going.

I don't care what happens. I remove her gag. "I'm so glad you're safe. I'm sorry, I'm so sorry."

She says, "I...I thought you guys were planning on hurting me." She looks from Gillian to me again and then down at her bonds. "You're not going to hurt me, right?"

"No, no...we just have to be sure you're you

again, sweetie," Gillian says, while I stand there stunned that Cassie could think I'd hurt her. She must know, after all we've been through, that I'd fight with every fiber of my being to never cause her harm no matter what Anat might do to me.

"Okay," she says, relaxing, words pouring out of her. "Would you mind getting these ropes off me, then? And what happened to me? I feel like the thoughts I was having were mine, but they were so...twisted. And Nat? That was really weird. Nat never does what anyone tells her to do. And she was all like, 'let me help you with that, dear' and 'what would you like me to do next'. Scary." She shudders. She's definitely my Cassie again.

I lift her out of the trunk and Gillian lays her hands on the wrist and ankle ties in turn. The bonds fall away.

"I'm sorry. I'm sorry we had to do this," I tell her, apologizing again. What else can I do?

"No, I know there's something going on. I can feel it. When I was in that trunk, it was like a haze lifted. I'm pretty sure I'm missing great big chunks of the last few days. And you two, you're not really..." She looks from me to Gilly, appraising. She shifts uneasily in my arms.

"No. There's nothing between us. What you saw was some kind of projection related to the dogs. Anat did it."

"Anat?" she questions, her brow furled. Her eyes turn to Gilly. "You got rid of Anat." Her eyes narrow, suspicion slipping over her face again before it relaxes back into curiosity.

Gilly says, "Sort of, sweetheart. She's definitely changed from what she was, even though her motivations apparently haven't. Tom didn't think there was any reason to tell you."

I take a deep breath, then say, "At the time, it seemed like a good decision. And I really thought I'd taken care of it."

"Okay, you guys have a *lot* of explaining to do, but first...." She kicks her feet and pushes against me with her hands. "You can put me down now, Tom. I have a killer headache. I need a nap."

I set her on her feet gently but reluctantly, and she follows Gillian, who heads into the house.

I expect her to set up house with me in my room now that she knows there's nothing up between me and Gilly, and Gilly does, too, I guess, when she leads her there to sleep. But when I rush into the room first to pick up the clothes I didn't bother to put in the hamper, she asks for her own room. She doesn't even glance at me. Gillian obliges her immediately, without a question.

Cassie doesn't care about the dirty clothes on the floor. Anat has played a winning hand again: even though I have her back where she'll be safe, Cassie still doesn't trust me.

I take out my wallet and check the all-important receipt is still there. I feel an urgent need to reassure myself it hasn't been magiced away somehow, too.

It's still there, and as long as it is, I know that ring will someday find a home on Cassie's finger.

***

"Don't leave me behind," Cassie says, her look pleading.

"You're safer here, Cass," I tell her. "We need to keep you hidden so Anat can't snatch you back."

"So, you're just going to leave me alone? Exposed?"

Gillian jumps in. "Hardly exposed, sweetheart. I can ward this room so well that the Goddess herself wouldn't be able to get into it. I've lived here so many years that my essence permeates the very walls. Any wards I place around it should be impassable."

Cassie looks doubtful. "But..."

I shake my head. "No buts. I know you don't trust me right now, and I don't blame you, because I made a bad mistake keeping you in the dark about what really happened to Anat, even if I did it because I thought it was best for you. But please believe me when I say it—I would rather lose my own life than put yours at risk. You'll be safer here."

She looks into my eyes, seeking, and I guess she finds what she's looking for.

"Fine," she says. "But I don't have to like it. What's so important that you have to break into Robert's place for it, anyway?"

"I forgot about the invisibility suit when I moved back to the shop. It's in a closet there. And it might help us find out what's going on."

Her face squinches, and her shoulders tense. I know she's thinking about where the suit came from: it was Kevin's, and he used it to peep on women, including Cassie. I start to move toward her for a hug, but her look tells me to stay where I am. Reluctantly, I step out of the room so the witches can do their thing.

Gillian wards the room from the hall as Cassie's quieter voice begins the chant to ward it from the inside after the non-magical lock tumblers click. Then, outside, Gillian does some more herb-burning and hand-waving around the perimeter of the house. That pup has no chance of getting to Cassie tonight.

Still, I'm distracted. It's not good enough to free Cassie from Anat. We need to free Robert and Natalie, too, before I can get off this adrenalin rush I'm riding.

***

"It's a little spooky out here in the middle of the night, isn't it?" Gillian asks, her words whispered and overwhelmed by the croaking frogs in the nearby pond, even though we're crouched in the damp brush so far out on Robert's property that there's no way he can hear us or spot us.

"It's the best time of night. The night things have woken up. I sense them around us." I sample the fragrant air in a long whiff and the musky animal scent fills my head with images of the hunt. "And smell them." I breathe a sigh of longing before I grab my senses back from Cat.

She looks at me a little surprised, her eyes wide in the scarce moonlight. "I guess I didn't realize how much of you is Cat even when you're you."

"He's a part of me." I shrug. And with only one of his lives left, he's a part I need to take good care of. My demon-goddess enslaver Anat or Eunice or whatever she wanted to call herself made sure of that when she tied my life to his.

"We're getting close to the first boundary." She stops for a minute, two fingers in the air, like she's pope-waving to her followers; she gestures with them from side to side. "It's just here and it's active...yes...oh my, that's clever." She beams with admiration. She just can't stop admiring Robert's handiwork.

She goes on, "It allows entry by a person's intent. Because we have no intent to harm the occupants of the house, we should be able to step through easily. Now, if Anat is actually in the house, well...that could create a problem. Because we certainly mean to harm her."

She steps forward again, slowly, and I follow.

"Yes, that's fine," she says. "As long as we don't mean harm to anyone within the circle, we should be able to pass through it at any time. You won't have trouble with this one tomorrow assuming that Anat still isn't present. And you have no intent to harm Robert or the pups?"

"Not so long as they have no intent to harm me. Getting a sense of anything else?"

"There are certainly other little traps here...." She suddenly flings an arm out to hold me back. The same movement a mother makes—my mother made—to keep her child safe when she slams on the brakes in traffic. "Don't step there," she says.

I stop dead in my tracks.

"I think that's an alarm. Magical sort, of course. Like a land mine but connected to a signal in the house instead of to an explosive device. It won't hurt you, but it'll let Robert know we're here. I expect there are more of those scattered about. Let me map out a path for you. You'll need to follow it precisely."

I stay put while she wanders, sometimes closing her eyes and, at others, reaching out through the air with her fingers wide, an intense look on her face. Gillian feels things other people can't feel, hidden things. If she wants to, she can discover all your secrets. If anyone can wrangle a way around Robert's wards, it's my ex-wife. It's not a power she likes to use, though. She says knowing people's secrets has turned many a witch in her family into a bitter old cynic. I can't really see that happening to Gillian.

I squat down to make myself less visible as Gillian explores. That may be a mistake. Cat's got my nose tilted up in the air, sniffing at the tantalizing fragrance of wildness that blows my way on the breeze. That's definitely a mouse. A tiny, furry, juicy, tasty mouse. My haunches tense, I gear up for the chase. And then I grab my body back from Cat's influence and stand up. "Gillian," I whisper. "Have you got enough yet?"

"Just a tick, Tom," she whispers back. All I see is a shadowy form twenty or so feet off, between me and the house, which is still half a football field away.

Looking out at Robert's house and land, it's easy to see he has done well in Giles. His house and its grounds are a showpiece, and now he's won Gillian, too. Yes, Robert has done very well for himself.

And you know what? Robert's no better than I am. He's made his mistakes in life, he wasn't perfect. And like him, I deserve a chance at a good life, too, with Cassie by my side. I was punished long enough. I paid my dues when Eunice held me hostage, and I became a better man.

Damn it! I've earned my right to slip that ring on her finger.

I give Cat back my nose and he sticks it into the air to breathe in the heady soup of animal scents in the dark. I'm better off leaving him in control of things right now. He never, ever feels one speck of self-pity.

I MEMORIZED THE MAP Gillian made last night during breakfast, darting glances at Cassie over the top, hoping for a smile or a sign she missed me, too.

Now, back at Robert's with Cassie safely warded into her room again, it's hit or miss whether or not I'm getting it right. I should have kept my attention on the map. When I veer a little out of line, I'm sure I hear a sharp intake of breath from behind the fence line where Gillian waits. It's midday now, and she crouches in the bushes to avoid being seen. There's nothing else out this way, but better safe than sorry. Beyond Robert's is forest land, leading off to Corey Woods. Secluded. Just the kind of situation you want if you're bent on breaking in and don't want to be discovered.

I make my way through the minefield. There's really no way to know if I've set something off, so from here on in, I need to scramble. For all I know, Robert is on his way home with the entire police force in tow.

I've got a handful of herbs to spread across one final barrier. Gillian says it should void the magic long enough for me to get in and the barrier would never hamper me from getting out. But if it doesn't work? I could be dragging myself out of here on broken legs.

I sprinkle. I need to just do it now. Take that step.

Seriously, I wish she hadn't told me what could happen. Because I'm really fond of my skinny gams exactly as they are.

I close my eyes and tense for it. I take the step.

My foot makes contact with the firm earth on the other side of the barrier. And then the other one joins it.

I let out a giant gush of the breath I didn't realize I was holding. Whew. Legs still intact.

I dance the bugaloo for a step or two, happy to have the boys still functioning, then I sprint to the house and try the back door.

Obviously, it can't be that easy to get in and get out with my prize. Gillian could get through the locks, but we agreed she needed to stay behind. If one of us gets caught, the other one of us needs to continue working on getting the others free, keeping Cassie safe, and trying to figure out what Anat has planned. Without magic, I'm obviously the least useful person in that plan.

Looks like I'm on my own with the breaking part of the entering. So, what the heck, I go for the obvious. I grab a decent-sized rock from the tidily kept bed around the foundation landscaping and pitch it through the window of the ground floor room where I stayed during Anat's possession of Cassie. At least this time around, Anat didn't take her with a full-blown possession. As difficult as it was to get her back, it was still a whole lot easier to get her out from under Anat's influence this time.

A not-so-magical alarm blares. I need to get in and out as quickly as possible now.

I pick the glass off the sill and away from the frame, then boost myself through when it's clear. There's no point in using Cat for this even though he could get in and out more quickly: I need to pick up my package and it's going to take a man-shaped me to carry it.

I head for the closet, and the "empty" bag I forgot to take with me when I moved back to the shop is still on the top shelf of the closet where I left it. I reach inside and pull out a hefty handful of nothing. I dress myself by feel, stepping in to the invisible coveralls, then I pull the hood and filmy face mask up over my head to hide myself completely.

Even if the cops burst in through the door now, they won't be able to identify me. Or see me. Or stop me from making rude gestures with both hands.

Man, I wish I'd had one of these things when I was in high school.

I pass a mirror and take a look. With the film attached to the coverall hood pulled down over my head, there's no one there.

I get back out through the window and sprint to where my partner in crime waits. I ignore the mines now. Who cares if a few more alarms go off? Everyone's already been alerted.

I spring across the fence and land heavily in the bushes near Gillian. She startles as the bushes part with a loud crackling sound. I lift my hood, wondering what my disembodied grin must look like. "Let's go."

We haul butt into the woods, heading for the unpaved turnaround where we left the car.

***

I'm making a couple of assumptions when I stroll into city hall in my Invisible Man suit. The first is that no one can see me. That one seems to be true.

The second is that city hall isn't somehow warded against invisible or magical threats. But I pass right along, ghosting by all the open doorways as I shadow along behind the Chief of Police. He's hurrying along the corridor toward the back— maybe going to Robert's office and maybe not. I'm as stealthy as Cat, treading lightly, silently. The suit makes me invisible, it doesn't make me inaudible.

Yes, Robert was the Chief's target, like I'd guessed. I saunter in behind as he enters the mayor's office. It's obvious Robert doesn't know I'm here, and his pup is napping next to the desk.

I've lucked out. It's possible animals aren't taken in by the suit because Cat can see it even though I can't. I don't know if other animals can also see it. Eunice might have created it specifically so that only Cat could see it as part of some long-term plan. Or, it might be visible to all non-humans. In that case, I hope demon doggy takes a long, long nap.

Because I always have luck like that. Sure I do. This will all go off without a hitch. All I have to do is stay completely silent and wait for Robert to blurt out Anat's nefarious plan to some evil co-conspirator.

I mean, that would be nice. But barring that, I'm looking for another chance to get the dog away from Robert and free him the way I freed Cassie.

***

I move to a position at the side of the room where I can see all the players easily—Robert, cop, and dog. If any one of them make a suspicious move, I need to know about it.

Robert rolls up a large paper he's had spread across his desk and greets the Chief saying, "I've been looking over the plans for the Faire, and it's sure to be successful if it goes as I think it will." He gets this odd look on his face then, mischievous almost. It makes my heart fall. It's not a look that belongs on Robert's face: my friend is not the mischievous type. As he places the rolled plans into a locked cupboard, he continues, "But first things first...did you find out what happened at the house?

"Your house is secure. It looks like the alarm scared the thief off. Nothing looks disturbed other than a broken window in one of the bedrooms on the ground floor," the Chief replies.

Giles's Police Chief is a skinny guy, and he's getting long in the tooth now, too, but I've seen him put a drunk twice his size in a headlock and take him down without even breaking a sweat. A guy's got to admire a thing like that. If I didn't know different, I might think he was drawing on some magical super powers. But he's just a non-magical who's really good at his job. He finishes his report with, "Of course, we won't know for sure that nothing's missing until you've been back there to check things out. You want me to leave the patrol on site?"

"The basement and study are still locked?"

"We checked those per your instructions. Still locked."

Robert motions to the officer to sit across the desk. "Thanks, Karl. I don't expect any further trouble."

I know the Chief has to have some knowledge of Giles's secrets. Enough to keep them to himself and cover up the worst of the witchy whoopses, as Nat calls them. I'd bet he owes Robert in some way. He sure seems devoted to him. I wonder idly if that would change if he knew that the small black pup sleeping just to the side of Robert's desk is actually calling the shots?

Robert settles into his own chair after the Chief settles in to his. "How's the force's prep for the Faire coming along?"

"We're ready. Excited about it. Our spouses are already making plans for what they'll do with the old Stanford place if they win. It's the talk of the town. The turnout is going to be huge."

Robert's head nods slowly up and down as he steeples his fingers in front of his face. His expression doesn't give a hint of emotion. "Everyone on the force needs to be there for something as big as this."

"Everyone's scheduled. Who could resist overtime pay heading into the holidays?"

"Excellent. One last thing, then. I'm sure your force won't object to a small celebratory drink beforehand?"

The chief's face opens up into a broad smile. "Can't think why anyone would. In the office before the event?" Robert nods to his question. The chief lifts his chin in acknowledgement. "We'll be here."

Robert stands up and walks around the desk. I expect him to head for a parting handshake. But instead he half-squats, half-bends down, looking uncomfortable—he's stuck with limited range of motion from arthritis that even the best magic hasn't been able to cure—and gives the sleeping dog beside his desk a scratch behind the ears.

Its eyes open in response.

And they snap straight to me. High-pitched yaps puts a fire under me as it springs to its feet.

I bolt for the exit.

Robert's tone is still even and emotionless when he says, "Scot, get the door. We've got a guest."

The door slams shut behind me. Too late. But I can hear the pup make it out just in time, too. His claws clack on the hallway tile as he follows behind.

I could scoop the stupid thing up, tuck it under my arm like a football, and slam dunk it into the cement sidewalk when I get across the goal line. But with a visible passenger, I could also get caught, trapped, and prevented from telling Gillian that it looks like the pain party Anat has planned is definitely going to go down at the annual Witching Faire.

I can't take this opportunity to try to free Robert. The pup gets a pass this time as I burst through the doors of city hall and barrel through the parking lot on my way to safety.

I don't stop to catch my breath until City Hall is no longer in sight.

"DON'T PUT THAT FLAP up when you talk to me. It gives me the willies when I look over and see your face hanging in thin air like that." I smile as I pull the suit's face film back down and Gillian drives on.

"If you kept your eyes on the road, it wouldn't be a problem."

"It's only natural to at least dart your eyes over when you're talking to someone." Which she immediately does. "Oh Goddess, that's worse. Anyone watching me will think I've taken to having conversations with invisible men."

I grin an evil grin. Which is, of course, completely wasted at the moment. "Is this when I remind you that you have?"

"Just get on with it." She rolls her eyes and her head twitches in frustration. "Since you've managed to leave Robert behind again, did you learn

165

anything?"

I sigh. I know she's worried about him. "Sorry, Gilly. And yes and no…not much. More than we knew before. He's going to have the entire police force into his office for a drink prior to the Faire, so I think we can pretty much count them out as being any help. I'd like to think a drink is just a drink, some good ol' boy bonding thing they always do before an event, but he's Kevin's father, after all, and way more powerful. Kevin kept the Giles police enthralled with his elixirs for years. Imagine what his high priest father can do with a flask of rum."

"Excellent point. Unless we can interfere with that somehow. It's something to put on the list, at least. Although the list is starting to get long. Anything else?"

"I think there may be an written plan for whatever it is Anat's got cooked up."

"Written?" She stops a little too quickly at a red light. We both bob forward in our seats. "Sorry. It's just that's exactly what Robert would do. He leaves a paper trail at breakfast. The man's a visual planner."

"That was my thought, but to know for sure, I'll need to get into a locked cabinet without leaving any evidence that I've been there to get it." We're far enough away from town hall now, so I peel the suit down off my shoulders, then sluff it off at my feet. I grab in the back for the bag and stick the suit inside so I don't lose it.

Gillian shakes an idea loose as the car squeals around a corner too fast and my head goes bobbing again. "Do you have any portable lock magic? Something that would work for anyone? Because I can't just walk in behind someone again."

Her brow furrows with thought. "I can cook something up even a non-magical could use. Easy peasy. Probably the simplest thing I'll have to deal with in all this mess. When do you plan on going back?"

"Tonight seems like a good time. The Faire is less than a week away now."

"We need to go to Salem for our necessaries, then, what with the Magical Shoppe being off limits. I haven't got everything I need to cook you up the right kind of charm for opening locks." She makes an abrupt right toward the road out of town instead of heading south to her place. "Goldenseal is relatively rare these days and not something I keep on hand. Even the Magical Shoppe only has a small store and practitioners have to ask for it."

I really want to call Cassie just to make sure things are okay with her, but her cell phone is still in her purse at the Magical Shoppe. First thing she noticed after she insisted on her own room.

"You think there'll be a place to pick up a temporary phone for Cassie on the way to Salem?" I ask. "I'd feel more secure if I could check on her and make sure she's okay when we're away like this."

Gillian nods. "We'll stop at the first place we see."

***

This place isn't set up as nicely as the Magical Shop, that's for sure, but Gillian says it's the best option for what we want. It's all t-shirts and haunted house snow globes at the front, junk for tourists. And in the next row, there are packets of ready-mix spices and crystals for playing at being a witch.

The real stuff will be in the back, under the heavy scent of incense and decay. Like a lot of Salem shops, you have to know someone to get it. Fortunately, Gillian knows everyone.

She tells the kid with the kohl-rimmed eyes at the counter what she wants, but she doesn't like the answer she gets back.

She leans in to rest on her arms, all smiles. "If Priestess Higgins says you're not to sell wild goldenseal without explicit permission from her, then I think you need to contact her and get permission."

"But she's taking the day off. I'm not supposed to bother her."

"I've known Lettie enough years to know that her bark is worse than her bite. You've noticed she's nearly toothless?" The girl's eyes widen in shock.

Lettie is missing a tooth in front, but wise people don't mention it if they value their health. Gillian continues, "And she certainly loves her profit. Tell her Gillian Winterforth has an urgent need for goldenseal. I won't even dicker on the price."

The girl hesitates, then picks up the phone and dials, carrying it back to the farthest end of the counter and turning away from prying eyes, whispering. The voice on the other end has no such volume control. It returns loud and angry. The shop girl has to hold the phone away from her ear while her boss rants.

Gillian fidgets at the counter, unconcerned, poking idly at a bowl of rodent skulls. Too bad they've been boiled so clean they are completely uninteresting.

The girl returns, looking upset. "Priestess Higgins told me to tell you, and I'm supposed to quote her..." The girl swallows hard. "...you can get your fat, aging hippie ass out of my shop before I come down there and blast it off for you."

"Fine. Tell her that I'm sorry I missed her."

Gillian heads toward the door, her head held high, and I follow her out.

"Great," I say. "I didn't know you and the High Priestess of the old Danvers coven were at odds. How are we going to get the goldenseal? Do you absolutely need it?"

"If I'm making you a portable unlock, I'll need it. But that won't present a problem." Gillian replies. "Lettie's been hostile to me since I cured her of one of those unmentionable problems that sometimes happens. When we were much younger, she didn't have the knowledge to manage it on her own." She shrugs. "You know how some people are when you help them out with an upsetting situation. They can't face you, so they make up a reason not to have to."

Then she reaches into her huge macrame handbag and pulls out a large jar labeled "Goldenseal" in antique lettering.

"When did you?" I run the events in the shop through my head again. No, there's no way she grabbed it when I wasn't looking. I was always looking.

"You think Natalie's the only one in town with a gift for finding things in her purse?"

I shake my head. "I had my eyes on you the whole time."

"Did you? Because I'm sure you must have blinked."

"Okay. It's not like I think you couldn't manage it. It's just I would have expected that from Nat. But you?"

"There's a fair payment for this jar sitting exactly where it was hidden behind the counter. So don't go accusing me of being a budding Natalie Taylor. Extreme situations call for extreme measures."

She's got that right. And, considering what's at

stake, I'm more than glad she's willing to to play free and loose with her moral guidance system.

***

After Gillian unwards Cassie's room, I put myself down for a nap and the girls head for the kitchen—I need it if I'm going to be alert when prowling around tonight.

What feels like only minutes later, I wake fuzzy-headed— although not literally, not furry-headed— I haven't yet taken up shifting in my sleep—to Gillian standing over me with a perfume atomizer full of a clear, amber liquid. Cassie is standing next to her. Our eyes meet for a long moment before hers slide away.

Gilly says, "You'll need to try this before you use it during this caper. I've locked the front door for you. It worked for me, but since I can pretty much open my own door just by thinking about it, you need to see if it works for you as well."

I yawn and sit up, then reach out for the bottle. She grabs the afghan I'd spent the last few hours under and folds it into a rectangle which she lays across the back of the couch and straightens to perfection. That's Gillian, tidying while the world ends. Based on the spicy smell coming from the kitchen, she's been baking something other than liquid unlock, too.

At the front door, I check to make sure it's

currently secured, then spray it with the fine mist from the atomizer and it glows briefly but nothing appears to happen. Despite it's sunny color, the mist smells like old machine oil. I look over my shoulder to Gilly. "Is there anything I need to say?"

"A 'thank you' wouldn't go amiss."

I lift one corner of my mouth in a wry half-smile and try the door. It's unlocked now. The stuff works like a champ.

I turn to give her a big hug. "Thank you. Sorry if I don't say that enough."

"No, I'm sorry I'm being so testy. I thought I understood what you went through when Anat possessed Cassie last summer, but I'd forgotten what it feels like to worry you're going to lose someone you love. I'd boxed all that up after I lost Martin. I never thought I'd be feeling that today for Robert. It's an awful, aching, angry pain...so you better find the answer to all of this and find it soon."

I tighten my hug at first, hold her in position too long, maybe, wanting to show her that I understand how important it is for us to get Robert back soon. But then I see Cassie looking at us, her blue eyes appraising. I let go. I let go fast. I don't want her to interpret my support of my friend the wrong way. Things are dicey enough between us right now as it is.

"I say it's time for us to get at it, then." I head for the mudroom to grab the invisibility suit and reach out to squeeze Cass's hand on the way, but she pulls it out of reach. There it is again, that grasping twitch around my heart. I don't really think she's worried about me and Gillian, but she might be upset because I left her in the dark about Anat.

I have to stay focused. Cassie will come around once the threat is gone. I know she will. I walk back to Gillian with the suit in hand. "You ready to be my getaway driver again?"

"It would be my pleasure."

I step into the coveralls by feel as Cassie and Gillian go upstairs to lock her up tight upstairs again. Soon, I'm all gone.

We're already on the way to City Hall before I remember I've still got the phone we'd bought for Cassie in the back pocket of my jeans.

GILES CITY HALL is buttoned up for the night. Only the exterior accent lights and intermittent lights in the downstairs burn, going off in one room and then coming on in the next as someone moves around the building. That's got to be the janitor. I watch for a while, and when the light travels to Robert's chambers then goes out again, I head to the back entry and mist the lock.

Bingo. I'm in.

I sneak down the hall not because I can be seen but because I can be heard. I don't need innocent bystanders gumming up the works tonight. It's terrible to admit, but I always enjoyed this part of being Eunice's familiar—it feels just like playing spy did when I was a kid. But that was a game, and what I'm up against now is very real. And very dangerous.

I apply more mist and the lock on Robert's door opens. Another spritz and I'm into the cabinet where I watched him store his rolled up plans. Gillian thought they might be warded or charmed. I hold the apophyllite crystal she gave me in front of the one last lock. It doesn't glow. There's no magic surrounding it. One final spritz and I'm in. That sure is sloppy on Robert's part. He would never get caught with his wards down like that if he was fully himself. Lucky for me that the evil Robert isn't on the ball to the same extent as his moral twin.

I grab the paper and unroll it. It's an artist's drawing of the downtown area where the Witching Faire will take place. It centers on the small downtown park and gazebo and pictures the shops and restaurants of downtown laid out around it. On each of the streets the locations of stands and stages are carefully marked out with information about what each one sells or is used for.

Clustered around the area where the streets will be closed off for the event, there are a series of large asterisks marked in red with letters and symbols next to them. It's done in Robert's chicken-scratch. He really should have been a doctor. But hopefully Gillian can make something of it.

Even though it's difficult to read, I can make out that one of the letters is a C crossed out and replaced with a question mark. For Cassie, maybe? Too bad we ruined whatever Anat had planned for her.

I smile to myself when I think of Cassie waiting safely at Gillian's.

Above the gazebo, there's a large symbol drawn in a circle, also in red. I haven't got a clue on that. It just looks like a scribble. But maybe the letters represent the witches Anat has under her control? This one could be an R for Robert. And this one? Could be a Z for Zelda. She has one of the pups.

I need to get a good image of this for Gillian. I've gotten better at taking pictures with this blasted traveling phone, tiny and ridiculous as it is—I can even usually manage not to take a picture of my own hand blocking the lens every other try—but I don't think it will give the detail we need.

I bet they've got one of those fancy electronic mimeographs around. What do they call them these days? A copy machine. Cassie has one hooked up to her computer, but she went to a shop to get the shop flyers copied in bulk. Pretty amazing that you could get them immediately. They used to take days at the printer. She told me that kind of thing is no big deal anymore and I need to "get out of the stone age". Yeah, like the sixties—the most vibrant time period of all time periods—had any resemblance to the stone age. But still, she says any decent-sized business office has their own machine for just that kind of thing. There has to be one around here somewhere.

But how am I going to get this long roll of paper down the hall without being noticed? If I stick it inside my coveralls to make it invisible, too, I risk wrinkling it and having Robert know someone has messed with it.

If I carry it down the hall out in plain sight, I risk the janitor freaking out over floating documents and calling someone to investigate. Or, at the very least, mentioning the strange sight to someone who'll tell Robert. Can't have that, either.

I roll up the plans and leave them on the desk, then take off without them to find the copy machine. Less chance of drawing attention that way.

I manage to find myself in a large room with what I'm looking for, although I'll never sort out how to use it with the only light coming from the snack machines. I'm going to have to wait out the janitor and come back with it when I can turn the lights on.

I go looking, and she's still puttering around through the offices, dumping a trash can here, taking a swipe with a rag at a windowsill there. She doesn't give it much more than a lick and a promise, and when she's done I follow her down to the basement where she takes the band out of her long, dirty-blond ponytail so that her thin hair falls over her shoulders, and then she sits on a folding chair, and puts her feet up on a handy box of cleaning supplies. She's got those tiny headphones they make these days stuck in her ears, and her eyes are glued to her phone screen as she pokes and prods at it.

This is my chance. She's on break or packing it in for the night. Either way, I scramble for Robert's chambers and the waiting plans.

The small room where the copy machine sits is at the building's center, but it still has windows to the hall that could give me away if I turn on the light.

In the dark like this, the infernal machine stymies me. Using a mimeo was simple—type your document up on a special sheet of paper, affix it to the wheel, and give it a crank until you have all the copies you need. I could do that in the dark.

Of course, I bet the monks all complained about having to learn to set type when the printing press came around. I was damned cool in my day: now I fear I really am the Neanderthal Cassie says I am.

I lift the lid and set the upper left quadrant of the plans on top of the glass face of the machine. That's how Cassie's scanner works, so I've probably done that right.

The buttons are lit. At least there's that. But it's too dark to tell what's written on them. And there's so blasted many of them. I hit one and it produces a beep.

Blast! It sounds like an airhorn in the silence. I go to the hallway and poke my invisible head out. But it's clear both ways.

I go back to the machine. There's more beeping, a flash of light around the plans that nearly blinds me—and a piece of paper—well, okay ten pieces of paper with identical copies burned onto them—spits out into a tray.

Ha! I just figured out how to get a copy out of this blasted machine! I'd like to see a Neanderthal manage that.

I hold up the image of the upper fourth of the map and it looks pretty good where there aren't spots in my vision. I flip the map around then, copying each corner as I go, until I've got the whole shebang. Neanderthal me even figured out what the lid was for this time. I fold the copies, unzip to my waist, and stow them inside my suit. All that's left is to get the set of plans back where they belong.

As I'm zipping the suit back up, the light changes in the hallway.

I freeze, halfway zipped, afraid to make a sound. All that's left is to get the rolled-up map back where Robert put it and let myself out with a spritz. I finish zipping in slow motion, keeping it as soundless as possible. Then, I poke my head out into the hall. The light is coming from the room next door. I sneak down the hall past it.

The janitor is bent over a garbage can when I dart across the doorway with my floating plans.

Once the plans are stowed again, I'm home free. I move more easily when I don't have to worry about creasing them or getting caught with them. I salute the cleaner when we walk past each other in the hall as I head to the front door.

***

Gillian's head is bobbing up and down over the wheel when I get back to the car as she starts to doze, then pulls herself awake. I peel off my suit in the darkness of the unlit alley she'd parked in and tap on the passenger side window to get her attention. She wakes with a start mid-bob, but she quickly orients herself and leans across the seat to unlock the door for me.

Her eyes move to the papers I stow on the dashboard. I stuff the invisibility suit into its waiting bag as she asks, "Is that it?"

"A copy. Hopefully, Robert won't be able to tell we've had a look at it. But I still have no idea what Anat's planning based on that map. Maybe you and Cassie will have better luck."

"I'm sure we will. Hopefully, it won't take all night for us to ferret out an answer. I haven't felt this exhausted since our last run-in with our dear friend Anat. I'm glad of the break between battles. I don't think I could have kept this up, going full tilt like this all the time." She yawns. "I have to admit, it's exciting, though." As she puts the car into reverse and starts backing out of the spot between two sets of dumpsters, she grins. "I guess I can't complain. How many women are still having adventures once they hit wrinklies stage?"

I shake my head. "No more adventures for me, thanks. When this is over, I want a quiet life with my beautiful wife and a couple of beautiful kids. I'll run my friendly local diner in what I hope turns back into a quaint, quiet town where nothing much ever happens, and I'll get fat and lazy in my old age." I pat my stomach to emphasize my point.

"In between Cat's hunting expeditions in Corey Woods, of course."

I see her point. But a guy can dream.

I SEALED THE DOOR from the inside and Gillian sealed it from the outside, so what could get to me, right? I'm not super thrilled that they keep leaving me behind while they work on figuring out what Anat's up to, but I mean, there's a window, my room here is on the second floor, and I watched Gillian standing underneath it, giving it some of her special-protection sauce before she went each time.

I'll be fine.

For real.

Okay, maybe I'll be bored: I should have made sure there was a TV in the room. Or something to read other than the local copy-shop-bound edition of The Young Witch's Guide to Auras that I grabbed off the bookshelf. Talk about making the supernatural seem tedious. It wasn't bad being stuck in here at bed time.

Okay, a nap? Maybe a nap? No, not until those guys get back. Auras it is.

Oh man, auras are boring. I drop the book on the floor and stare at the ceiling. Yep. Nothing much going on up there.

I'm glad I have my own room despite the lack of entertainment, but when I think how Tom looked when I told Gillian I didn't want to share...well, he crumpled up like I'd hit him in the stomach or something. There's that place where if you get hit there, you can't breathe for a while and you think you're going to suffocate until your lungs start functioning again. That place and that kind of hit. He crumpled forward a little, and he looked like he was in pain.

I felt sorry for him. But I still flash to that picture I have of him and Gillian trying to suck each other's tongues out. I mean, I need some time to process that it didn't really happen. Right? It seemed so real. It's still hard to believe that a bunch of cute little puppies arranged themselves around town just to put on a show for me.

The problem is, that, just like me and Dan, those two are each other's first loves. He's never going to forget her, no matter how old she's gotten. I don't think he even cares about that—I bet he still sees her as the girl he married a g-zillion years ago. I know he does. He doesn't see her as a white-haired granny lady.

And I guess that's good. If he and I do end up

together, he'll see me that way when we're old, too.

If he gets old, I mean. If Cat doesn't run up against a raccoon with an attitude or not see a car coming when he's crossing the street. Because he's only got the one life left now. He gave up number eight for me, to save me from Anat. Which is okay, because one life is kind of the normal number. Better than none, at least.

Anyway, I've got to get over this icky, stuck visual of Tom and Gillian together. I want to. My brain knows it isn't true, but my heart...

There's a noise outside and my wary heart skips a beat, revving on adrenalin at the sound. It's a squeaky little bark. A Blackie kind of bark. I don't want to look, but I have to.

I feel weighed down as I move to the window and look out to the front yard. Blackie is there, his pink tongue lolling out the left side of his mouth as he stares up at the window. His tail wags furiously when our eyes meet.

He's come for me.

And he's not alone. He's brought friends. Zelda and her daughter Deborah are with him, accompanied by a pup of their own, whose tail is also pumping away now, just as happy to see me.

I'm everyone's favorite: if Zelda and Deborah started wagging their behinds to the doggy rhythm, I wouldn't be surprised. It's like they're one unit, sharing one thought. They all stare up at me with the same vacant look in their eyes.

Looking back down at them, it's kind of calming, you know? Sweet of them to come to visit...

OMIGOD!

I snap out of it and tear myself away from the window. I hope Gillian warded the door to keep me from opening it, because that was my next thought—I was going to open the door and go out to meet them. I hope she remembered this time. As long as she doesn't die or something, she can always let me out.

Why am I thinking about Gillian dying? And why doesn't it bother me to think about it? That wouldn't be right even if she was grinding all over Tom right now. And, ew...I am trying not to think these things, so why am I thinking these things?

My little Blackie is so cute, you know? And I really want to go down and scratch behind his ears and maybe throw a stick for him to chase. Who cares about Tom and Gillian? They can have each other. I turn the knob, but the door stays shut tight.

OMIGOD!

I snap out of it and back away from the door. My heart pounds. Thank the Goddess that Gillian thought to keep me safe from myself. I cover my ears to drown out the high-pitched yapping from outside and try to think. What can I do?

I'll just go look out the window for a second to see if I can figure anything out.

I stand at the window and yes! Tom and Gillian

are back. They'll take care of it, I'm sure.

But they're just standing there.

Holding hands.

And now they're turning to each other...wait a minute...Gillian doesn't seem to have an actual backside? Tom's hand is squeezing a handful of missing butt cheek like there's something there. And part of the top of Tom's head is missing. You can see right through it to the grass behind him.

I pull my eyes away from that scene, and the two pups are standing on either side of it, their eyes glowing faintly red, like demonic film projectors.

I open the window and shout, "Get the hells bells out of here, all of you! You're not welcome!"

Because sure, that'll take care of it, right?

Both pups look up at me then, and the apparition of the lovers disappears. I feel a little woozy but also drawn to the group waiting outside. I pull a leg up and lift it over the sill. I can step out onto that little bit of roof over the entryway, and then from there, I should be able to sort of slide off into the bushes, which should break my fall.

OMIGOD!

I snap out of it and look for something I can use to try to scare them away. There isn't much. Bedding. A small desk. A bunch of linens and winter coats in the closet.

So, I rifle through the desk and come up with a couple of packs of ball point pens, stationary, and an eraser. I guess I could always write a stirring speech about how I won't be taken.

Or, if I had some kind of bow, I could make ballpoint pen arrows and declare war.

You know, that's not a bad idea. I wonder if I get creative with some of the magic that I already know I could launch a pen toward a target. And there *is* something I know. I think it through—yes, it's the right kind of energy, I think. It's a simple repelling charm, but if I get it right and can sort of aim it, I think I could shoot a pen in their general direction. I'd have to put enough oomph into it that it would hurt when it hit, though. Enough that they'll think there's some real danger.

It could work. Or I could just run out of pens while they stand there beaming badness at me. Not like I was going to write that speech anyway, right?

I stand at the window and put the blunt end of the pen against my palm, then focus on pushing it outward. I don't blink. I can't take my eyes off it as it flies toward its target. I have to guide it.

It's really moving. This could work.

Nice! It smacks Zelda just below the knee, and she bends down, her hand moving to the spot, giving a little cry. I can't tell if it's surprise or pain.

Time for another shot. I aim for Blackie this time. And again, it's going right for the target, but…oh Goddess, oh no.

Oh horrible. Horrible, horrible horrible.

Blackie drops, blood seeping out of his left eye where the pen went in deep. His howl is low and awful.

I can't look. I cover my eyes and back away from the window.

The pull has stopped, though. I can't feel their presence dragging at me anymore.

I risk another look out the window. Blackie's little body is alone out there, not moving.

I collapse on the bed, tears gushing into the lumpy chenille spread. He was just an innocent little puppy. None of this was his fault.

***

The tears stop when the crashing sounds of demolition in the hallway start. They can't have broken through the wards on the doors downstairs, can they?

Yet the sounds of objects hitting the walls, plaster tearing away, and a humming coming from the door tell me they have. I know that sound. It's the sound of magic thrumming against the the wooden surface. I bet one or both of the witches are trying to open a hole through it. It's what I'd try if wards wouldn't let me open something.

Leaving a loophole like that would be novice witch stuff, though, and Gillian's no novice. She's got that door and all the walls around this room sealed, locked, and overcoated. The windows, too.

But that's what I would have said about all the ways to get into the house. If they can break those wards, they might be able to break the ones up here, too.

My heart races knowing that they're only feet away from me and done with being subtle.

I back into the farthest corner of the room and slide down to the floor. My arms hug my knees, and I work to calm myself.

No, wait...why am I acting so helpless? That's stupid. There's got to be something I can do that doesn't involve cowering in a corner. I've helped beat Anat twice before. I am so far from helpless. Now that I know what I am, as long as I've got sleeves, I'll always have tricks up them. I'm not a frightened kid: I'm a witch!

The mother and daughter bwitches shout my name, telling me to come out or they'll tear the house apart to get me. I press my hands over my ears, refusing to listen to their threats.

And it comes to me; I know what I can do.

I've got something I can use that only a powerful witch could pull off: I think it can get them to back off, or at least hold them off without killing anyone. And I think I can project it through the wards.

I step out of the corner, bring my magically-charged hands down from my ears, and shove them out forcefully in the direction of the door. I hear two loud thumps and a smaller one as three bodies hit the wall at the end of the hall.

I was thinking too small before. I can repel a lot

more than a pen.

I hear footfalls charging down the hall as they come back at me, their wails now laced with rage, and I hit them with another wall of wham-bam.

I keep taking out their charges until there's silence behind the door. I don't let myself believe yet that it means they've gone. I also don't let myself believe I've bashed all of their brains out against the back wall of the hallway, because it's too terrible to think of.

At least with the silence, I can relax a little, rubbing at a shoulder and the back of my neck to massage the knots. But it's no good. My body is still tense and ready. All I can do until Gillian gets back to let me out of here is hunker down to wait and hope the attack doesn't start up again

"TOM! THE HOUSE..." Gillian gasps as the car rounds a corner and her home comes into view. The front door stands open. When the car pulls into the driveway, my feet hit the ground, and I'm halfway to the front stoop before the car pulls to a full stop.

I force myself to breathe as I pound toward the stairs that lead to Cassie's room. As I climb, my boot heels crunch shards of glass from the pictures that once lined the walls.

At the top, as I enter the hall and turn toward Cassie's room, it's even worse. The door to the room is blackened, sooty, but still standing. The hallway isn't in very good shape. There's not a picture left hanging and the plaster is full of holes, large and small, some breaking all the way through to the next room.

As I move toward the end of the hall, pushing aside clumps of plaster and lath, the plaster dust drifts into the air, and I sneeze, but I keep on going.

"Cassie?" I call, as I reach the door, laying my hands on it, then taking them off quickly when I realize the door isn't just sooty, it's hot. Really hot. "Cass?"

"Tom?" comes her response, quavering.

"You okay?"

"Yes. Get me out."

"I can't. But Gillian's coming. She was behind me." And she is; I hear her breathing heavily as she rushes up the stairs. And then she gasps when she steps into the devastated hallway.

I turn, and she's picked up one of the ruined pictures from the floor—a wedding picture of her and her deceased husband Martin, the good husband, the one that wasn't me, and for a moment I'm sure she'll cry. The picture is ruined. Bits of glass have scratched it beyond repair.

But she sets it down and moves quickly toward me, her face composed now.

"Is she okay?" she asks.

"She says she is. But she wants out."

Gillian does a complicated maneuver that involves some hand-waving, the sprinkling of an herbal concoction from her purse, and a few words I don't catch, then reaches for the door handle and opens it easily. I squeeze around her into the room.

Cassie runs into my arms.

"I'm so sorry that I ever doubted you, Tom. I get it now. Those stupid, stupid dogs tried to trick me again, but they didn't fool me a second time."

She unclasps me and goes to Gilly, enveloping her now, too. "And I'm sorry I doubted you, too. I know you better than that. I'm sorry I thought the terrible things about you that I was thinking.

Gilly rubs Cassie's back soothingly, then parts from the hug.

"I'm glad you've forgiven us, sweetheart," Gillian says as she takes in the destruction in the hallway one more time with a turn of her head. "Because Tom's room doesn't have a wall anymore. I expect he'll be needing a more private place to sleep."

***

We begin work to clear up the mess in the hallway, and Gillian tries not to show how upset she is, but I can tell she is one droplet away from letting go a waterfall. When Cass finishes telling us what happened and how she finally got her attackers to clear out, I tell Gilly, "Look, Cassie and I can do this for you. You don't have to help."

"What would I do? Pretend this didn't happen until you have it semi-respectable again? Pretend it doesn't hurt me that my precious images of Martin are gone forever? I knew I should have had them put on disk or that cloud thing all the young people talk about, but I just never got around to it."

I'm not certain I know what she means by a disk, and putting pictures on a cloud? Is that some new witch thing? But nobody understands regret better than I do. "I want you to feel better," I say, dropping my eyes to the plaster-covered floor, my shoulders drooping, "And I don't know how to help."

"I'll feel better when Anat is out of our lives for good."

Cassie drops a piece of broken glass into the trash can. It chimes as it joins the inch of broken glass already in there. "I second that. And by the way, you two are *not* leaving me out of your plans again."

"No, we bloody well are not," Gillian agrees, her hands on her ample hips, surveying the hallway for her next task. "We'd be fools to lock you up for your safety. It's clear you can take care of yourself. I could never have used that spell to throw two people and a dog down a hallway at the same time."

Cassie shrugs. "I was motivated."

"I think we've found your talent—I wonder if any of your ancestors were warrior witches. If that's the case, remind me never to motivate you. "

Cassie gives her a big smile. "A warrior witch, huh? I did think about ending both of you when I thought Tom was doing the dirty on me."

I look up at her, my eyes wide. Gilly's mouth gapes.

"Seriously, guys?" She laughs when she sees our look of alarm. "Like it's in me to be a killer. Except, you know, Blackie..."

I put a hand on her shoulder gently. "I didn't want to say anything about the dog on the lawn."

Her lip quivers, and she lets loose a big, gasping sigh. "That was an accident. I just wanted them to go away."

Gillian and I look at each other. I know the question she wants to ask. I want to ask it, too.

I try not to sound harsh, but Cassie has to hear it. I say, "You know we may have to kill all of the pups, right? And the mother dog, when we find her? We can't risk Anat still hanging around."

"I know it, but...."

"But what if it comes down to you or them?"

She looks me in the eyes after blinking away the last of the wetness. "If that's the case—if it's me, or you, or Gillian, or Robert, or anybody I care about, that crew is dead doggie meat.

I PUT THE PIECES of the map together and tape them in place so that it matches the way I first saw it in Robert's office.

"Was any of this in color?" Gilly asks, as she looks over my shoulder.

"Yes, some of the lines and letters that were drawn over the top."

She goes to a big, oak buffet and rummages through the drawers, then returns and hands me a set of colorful felt tip markers. "I hope you were thinking like a warlock at the time and made a mental note of them?"

"Sure, I think I got 'em."

I color in the five asterisks around the edges of the map in red. Then I fill in the colors of the letters written next to four of them, as close as I can remember it. A fifth asterisk has no adjoining letter.

When I'm done, I point out the letters. "I think these are initials for each of the witches Anat has under her control. Is that a Z there? If so, that would be for Zelda…and that could be a D or maybe an O? And that's an R, right?" I look up for confirmation, and both Cassie and Gilly are nodding their heads. "R could be for Robert. And the C, that would be for Cassie, I bet…" I share a look with my girlfriend when I say her name. Her look is intense, serious. "…crossed out at the top with a question mark next to it. But I don't see an N for Natalie. Maybe that's what will replace the question mark."

I move my finger across the page. "Or maybe an N will go over here where there's no initial. And then at the center—what's that scribble anyway?"

Gillian pulls the map to a spot on the table before her and brings her hands to her mouth, her fingers folded slightly into each other as she makes a steeple in front of her lips. It's almost like she's praying, but I know she's only thinking. It's a gesture she's picked up from Robert, something recent. It comforts me. It feels like Robert is in the room, lending his support.

After a long interval, she says, "That could be a J for Janice. I haven't talked to her for a while. I felt a little guilty after having to drug her during the…well, you know…so I don't know if she's under Anat's influence or not." She takes a deep breath and blows it out loudly. "I hate to admit it, but I wish Natalie was here. She has a keen mind. If there's a pattern there, she'd see it. But if Natalie was going to replace her, I'd think they would have drawn that in. They had her before they lost Cassie." I've been nodding away during this. It all makes sense, and I can't think of anything to add.

"May I?" Cassie asks, gesturing to the map. Gilly pushes it toward her, and Cassie turns it around to orient it toward her. It makes just about as much sense upside down as it did right side up.

Cassie twirls a long strand of brown hair around her finger while she stares at the map, her cheek moving like a pregnant woman's belly as her tongue swirls around the inside of her mouth as she thinks. It's adorable. Who cares what's happening on the map? I want to take her up to our room right now.

I imagine bursting into flames to get focused on something other than Cassie's glossed-pink lips that I can't kiss right now. Doesn't work at all.

"What do you guys think this is?" She points to what looks like a random scribble. "Why does that look familiar?"

I grab the map and turn it around, taking a closer look. "Sheesh. It's a hieroglyph. Badly drawn, but it's a hieroglyph." I take a closer look at the map. "And there's definitely a couple more..." I point to their locations. "...here, here, and maybe here. I think that's it."

"What do they mean?" Cassie asks.

I point to the one near the crossed-out C. "This

one means love. And that one…" I point to the one near the letter R, "…that definitely means judgment. The others, I don't know."

Cassie says, "Do you think that the witches themselves symbolize something she plans on using for a spell? I mean, Robert is high priest and mayor, so he will sometimes stand in judgment of others, right? And me…" She looks up at me with a grin, her eyes flicking shyly to the side, "Well, Anat is really pissed that you love me and not her. At least, that's the sense I got from having to share my body with her. She never said or thought that concretely, but the feel of it was definitely there."

"Oh Goddess, I can't believe I missed this," Gillian says, springing up from her chair to go back to the sideboard. She returns with a ruler and picks up a pencil from the table. Then she lays the ruler down from one of the initialed asterisks on the map and draws a line. She repeats the lines until what she's drawing emerges.

I say, "Yep. Looks like you found yourself a pentacle."

"And…" Gillian says, "the body of the pentacle is almost dead center in the middle of downtown. What Cassie said—there will be something symbolic about it. It has to be a pentagram she's building for a particular ritual. And I bet that's where we'll find Anat when whatever she's planning happens."

"So, we're talking loosely Cat's Magical Shop,

the Diner of Earthly Delights, the Giles Gallery of the Arts, Twinkle Trinkets, Bountiful Bakery, that cluster of shops?" I point to each on the map as I confirm.

"The gallery! Omigod." Cassie slaps a hand over her mouth and sucks air through it. Gillian and I both look over and wait for the follow up.

"You guys, I know where Anat is. She's got to be downstairs in the gallery." She reaches over and squeezes my hand. "I never told you about my weird experience that day because you were all excited about Robert offering you the diner."

"What weird experience? What day?"

"I thought the boss was doing some furry role-playing with his boyfriend because I heard growling from the secret room downstairs. I mean, it was kind of scary until I decided it was playtime, but...well, I didn't think it would be Anat, you know what I mean?" She looks around for support. "And when I was all fuzzy-wuzzy instead of acting like myself, I think Dash and Jon were spending a lot of time down there." She bites her lip, face tense, thinking. "Yeah, they were definitely in the basement a lot, and there was this feeling I had that there was something down there that was important. But, well...I'm not clear on details and it just never occurred to me..."

Gillian reassures her when her voice trails off, saying, "There was no reason to think it was her, sweetie. As far as you knew, she was gone. We kept things from you. We all thought she was out of the picture."

"I know…yeah, I know…and then Blackie got to me…." Her look is a mixture of sadness and disgust when she says the pup's name, but she shakes it off. "Anyway, it's not like I was thinking straight."

"No, you weren't, and I'm not sure I would have thought anything different than you did if I'd been in the gallery with you," I say, then put my attention toward the map again. "If it's true Anat's been in the gallery, then I hope this one that is probably a D is Deborah—that's Zelda's daughter's name, right?—and not Dash. I don't see how Anat could use him in a spell anyway—he's never displayed any magical tendencies, has he?"

Gillian shakes her head. "No. Nor Jon, either. They're both still out-of-towners by Giles standards even though they moved here years and years ago."

"Good," I say. "So it looks like we've identified some of the major players and their locations. Although I still wonder where Nat will be in all of this. And we need to figure out what these hieroglyphs…" I say as I point to the scribbled pictographs in the center and at the remaining asterisks "…mean for us."

"The problem is that she's using ancient middle-eastern magic, which no one in Giles knows anything about, and she's got the one person who might have a shot of figuring it out under her influence," Gillian says.

My brows furl as I shake my head. "Not the only person who could figure it out, Gillian. You're every bit as powerful as Natalie."

"As powerful, yes. As knowledgeable about casting, no. Natalie has devoted nearly every waking moment of her life to magic. I had other things to do. But I wasn't talking about Natalie; I was talking about Robert—he's studied the arcane for fifty years. Plus, Natalie…"

Her face drains suddenly of color as her sentence peters out.

"What is it?"

"Natalie's magic is at its strongest at Samhain."

"So?" I ask.

"Do you remember why the Giles coven stopped using the old ritual grounds in the woods and moved to the newer one?"

"Some guy in the thirties brought his wife back from the dead, right?" I shrug. I don't know what ancient coven history has to do with it.

"Yes, he pulled her essence back from the Summerlands, or perhaps even from her next life, and into a rotted corpse."

I hear Cassie's quiet, "Yugh," as Gillian pauses.

"That was Natalie's grandfather. Her family has always had a special affinity for death magic just like mine has an affinity for secrets and hidden things, but you don't want to bring it up with her. After the zombie incident, the town shunned the family for a long time."

"So, why did you go white as a ghost yourself for a minute there?" I ask.

"Tom, the Witching Faire is held on Samhain. Non-magicals think of it as a Halloween celebration, but it's not. It's a celebration of the new year, the day when the veil between this world and the Summerland is the thinnest. The Faire ends early in the evening so we'll have time to gather for the Sabbat ritual afterward. And Samhain is the day when Natalie's powers, which reside between the worlds, are at their most powerful."

Cassie sighs a long sigh, "Ohhhhhhhhhh...that is so not good." I look from the young witch to the old one. They're obviously thinking something I haven't caught on to. And they both look worried.

Gillian says, "Exactly. Anat's own magical power is greatly diminished by the lack of a magical host, but if she's got Natalie's annual power boost to draw on..."

Oh. I get it now. Natalie's sorcery-on-steroids just turned into sorcery-on-steroids-on-PCP.

I reach for Cassie's hand over the table and squeeze it tight. Then Cassie and I both reach out for Gillian's hands and we stay like that for a long moment before Gillian breaks it up by reaching for the tea things to clean up.

***

Cassie moves to my side of the coffee table and sits between my legs so I can rub at the knots in her neck. I doubt I'm doing much good, no matter how skillfully I knead. Cassie says, "Mmmmmmmmmm," as I press my thumbs in at an especially tight spot, but no matter what she says, her body is saying, "Forget it." The knots stay knotted.

Gillian returns from the kitchen after disposing of the tea service, talking excitedly, "Doug says he'd be glad to take a look at the hieroglyphs. Let me just grab some pictures and send them to him."

She snaps pictures with her phone, stopping between each snap to email it off to the university Egyptologist in Boston who helped us out with the symbols on Anat's Ab Khr, the box that held her soul between bodies.

"What if he tells Robert? They're buddies right?"

"You think I wouldn't think of that?" Gillian says, adding a "tsk" on the end. "I told him that I'm preparing a surprise for Robert's birthday, which is quite factually coming up next month, so he won't say anything."

"Perfect." I push my thumbs across Cassie's tight shoulder muscles one last time before giving up and ask, "Do you need us? We…"

She looks up from her phone and smiles. "Oh no—you two can run along for a while."

Cassie holds my hand as she pulls me up toward her room, the only one upstairs that doesn't have holes in the wall from the witch's assault.

Once we're inside, I pull her close and our lips sink into a long, loving kiss, hungry for what they've missed. I stop worrying about us as her mouth glides across mine. There's no hesitation there: she no longer has any doubts about my loyalty.

I place my hands on the sides of her face and reluctantly move her lips away from mine long enough to whisper, "I promise I'll never keep you in the dark again. You and I together, we'll always beat anyone who tries to tear us apart."

We look into each other's eyes for a long moment, then she reaches to the side of my face.

"Always," she whispers back. "You and I are unbreakable. "

Our lips move together again, soft, then urgent. I kick the still half-open door closed with a backward thrust of my foot, unwilling to let her go. She moves back, her hands sliding to grasp my own firmly as she steps backward toward the bed, pulling me along with her. Neither of us wants to break the bond of touch, so we don't. Not for a long time.

***

An hour later, I brush Cassie's silky long hair aside to land a kiss on her shoulder as she playfully struggles against me, trying to get dressed so that we can find out if Gillian's found anything out about the symbols.

So, hang on, wait a minute—that's new. I've memorized every single square inch of Cassie's body, and this blue symbol? Not there before.

"What's this mark here?" I ask.

"What mark?" Cassie replies.

"On the back of your neck. Did you get a tattoo?"

"No. Let me look." She pulls her hair to the side and backs up to the mirror over the dresser. Her lips and brows scrunch in concentration. "That looks like the hieroglyph on the map, doesn't it?"

"Exactly like that." I'm an idiot. I'm trying to decide if girl tattoos are sexy when I should be thinking   evil-mark-put-there-by-a-demon.   I continue, "And this is the one for 'love', now that I'm looking at it with my brain instead of my..." I don't need to finish the sentence because she giggles. Then her face darkens, and she squeaks out, "Tom? Get it off. Getitoffgetitoffgetitoff."

"Yes. We need Gilly. Now."

***

Gillian's face is a mask of concern as she inspects Cassie's bare neck with her reading glasses low on her nose. She runs a finger along the mark, then bends down and swipes her tongue across it.

Cassie jolts forward. "What the..."

"Sorry, sweetheart. I got into detective mode and forgot to warn you. Sometimes you have to use all senses to investigate, don't you?"

Cassie looks over her shoulder, her lips quirked like she might laugh any minute. "Fine, then. Whatever. Just give a girl a warning next time. What's the verdict?"

"I *think*, although I can't say for certain, that it's exactly what Tom thought it was. It's a tattoo of sorts. But one created with magic rather than needles. That would be why you didn't know it was there. I think it's purpose was to track you, which obviously worked."

"So, how do we get rid of it?" Cassie asks.

Gilly takes a deep breath. "We could try to draw the magic out. Like a boil. But we'd have to have something else living to transfer it to for that to work."

My eyes move to Polly's cage in the corner of the room. Gillian's eyes track mine. "Oh, no you don't. Not Polly. And then what would we do, anyway? They'd still think Cassie was here because Polly is."

And then I have the perfect idea. "You work on the spell. I'll bring you just the thing."

After a brief investigation through the cupboards, I go out the back door with an empty mason jar, set it down on the stairs, and take off the lid so Cat can drop his catch in when he gets back. Then I take a quick look around to make sure none of Gillian's neighbors are spying over their fences, and I shift.

It's brief. It's painful. But I emerge smaller, swifter, and completely unconcerned about neighbors or modesty or anything other than the enticing scents of the neighborhood wildlife. I flash away across backyards and under fences, sniffing the air for the scent of the one that will be the best match for what I need.

Cat won't be happy when I have to hold him back from the kill.

WHEN TOM GETS BACK, he comes walking out of the kitchen with a live mouse in a Mason jar. That would explain the clattering around in cupboards he did before he left. I wonder how hard he had to fight to get Cat to drop the poor thing instead of killing it and having it for dinner.

Tom sets the jar on the table, and I get down on my knees to take a closer look. At least it doesn't look injured. Its tiny, fragile-looking paws scrabble at the side of the glass and its black eyes are bright, its whiskers quivering as it sniffs the air. It's so cute! It kind of reminds me of Dash when he's nervous, which is a lot of the time.

I hope transferring my tattoo to it won't hurt it. I'm feeling all kinds of bonded with it now.

Gillian asks, "Ready?"

I guess I am. I pull my hair aside to bare my

neck for the herbal glaze and parchment we'd prepared. It should draw and hold the magic until Gillian can place it onto the mouse.

She says, "Just one last thing. Tom, could you hold the jar for me while I prep the mouse?"

He holds it up toward her, and she sprinkles a few herbs inside, chanting softly under her breath, watching the mouse intently. Its eyes close and it slowly sinks to the floor of the jar, its frightened movements stilled.

"You didn't kill it?" I ask.

Gillian shakes her head. "No, sweetness. It's just sleeping. I need to shave a little spot so there's some bare skin available. Tom, would you lay it out on the table for a moment?"

Tom is gentle with the mouse as he tips the jar and the poor little thing slides down the side of it into his big, outstretched palm. I bet he's fighting Cat's every instinct on that one. Cat would definitely not be gentle.

He sets the mouse on its side on the table, and Gillian carefully runs an electric razor over it until its bare, pink skin is exposed. "It should sleep for at least another ten minutes. That should be plenty of time."

The herbal glaze bites down cold on my neck when she slathers it on, and the muscles Tom loosened up in our bedroom contract again in protest. As the magic is drawn out, it feels like dull needle pricks. I bet a lot of people wished they could be un-tattooed this easily. Gillian could make a tidy profit in the broken romance market.

She places the parchment and smooths it down onto the magical ooze, then writes on it with a piece of charcoal. After she pulls it away from my neck with the gel still stuck to it, she brings it around in front, so that I can see she drew a picture of the hieroglyph. Instructions to the magic, I guess: remove this but leave the rest.

She smooths the parchment onto the mouse's skin and says a few more words under her breath. Then she carefully removes the charcoal from the paper with one of those art erasers you can smoosh into different shapes by dabbing at it gently, kneading the eraser to get a clean spot, and then repeating.

She obliterates the symbol soon enough, and the parchment is as clean as it's going to get. She pulls it away from the mouse's body.

Underneath, the symbol that was once on my neck is now on the mouse. Tom picks the sleeping mouse up just as gently as he laid it down and helps it slide softly down into the bottom of the jar by tipping it ever so slowly until it stands upright.

"That's it?" he asks Gillian.

I show him my neck.

"Clean as a whistle." He says, as he plants a kiss where the tattoo had been. "So, I'm off to take this guy back to where I found him. I left a decent distance between here and the house before I started the hunt. It shouldn't lead anyone back here. I'll make sure he's awake before I dump him out. He won't be much of a decoy if something has him for dinner as soon as I drop him off. But hopefully, if they're still tracking you, they'll think we've moved you. And even if they don't, you'll be where we are from now on. They'll have to take us all on if they stake out the house. Although, I think we should probably move our base of operations once this is done."

And then he's gone into the night again, but this time as my handsome, manly Tom, always there to be my white knight. Not that I need one, right? But I have faith we can win any battle together and have our relationship come out even stronger at the end.

No, I don't care how many enchantments anyone throws at me, I'm never going to doubt Tom again.

***

Gillian and I are packing the basics of what we'll need when we bug out for the cabins my Granny owned in Corey Woods. It's a good idea just in case the doggy crew keeps the house under surveillance despite the mouse trick. Her phone chimes, and she looks at it, then gives me a big grin. "Doug has all of the translations sorted already."

She grabs a pen and writes the translations on

the map next to each corresponding hieroglyph.

I sit down to take a look, and when I get to the one in the center, a bad feeling runs up my spine and does a couple laps around the inside of my head.

"Underworld?" I ask her.

"Underworld." She replies.

"What do you think that means?"

"It can't be good." She sits quietly for a minute, her face a blank, then bounds up, heading for the kitchen. She calls over her shoulder, "Tea?" before she's out of sight.

Yep, we better pack a lot of tea. I put it on the list.

Then I cycle through the translations again. Love, death, judgment, power, chaos, and finally, underworld. Right at the center.

A lot of possibilities go through my mind. I'm not far enough along in my studies to be sure, but my brain is definitely spitting out ideas.

I've been reading up on witchy stuff lately, and Samhain is the very best time to hold a seance and talk to your dearly departeds. Or to raise someone from the dead. Or to make a zombie. And Natalie, who comes from a family of witches who can probably easily do all those things, and who is uber-juiced with magic on that one night, is under the control of Anat, the bitch-goddess who hates us all.

Gillian reenters the room just in time to hop on the nightmare express with me. When she sits down, I watch her face closely. If she shows fear, we're really in for it.

"So, is Anat up to something that has to do with how thin the veil between the worlds is on Samhain, do you think?"

Her face shows me exactly what I was looking for. I can feel the already tight knots in my neck tying themselves into super-knots.

"I'm afraid so, sweetie. All of the indicators are there. What is it that you young people say?" Her eyes flick up to the right briefly as she searches for the words. She finds them easily enough.

"We are so screwed.

Tom snugs up against my back with his arms tight around me as we watch Gillian frying up breakfast on an old, but adequate camp stove. We've taken over a couple of the better cabins that sit side by side, and it has been comfortable without any disturbances. The heating situation isn't great, though, with only a small space heater that we brought from Gillian's in each cabin. We've had to snuggle close for warmth at night. It's been awful. Really.

I relax into him, figuring this is probably my last opportunity to be something other than a knotted up mass of anxiety today. With the Witching Faire tonight and everything we're going to have to try to accomplish to free our friends and keep Giles safe, it will be a while before I can lay back into his arms again.

"Tell me what you think will happen if we don't break the lines of power tonight?" Tom asks Gillian. "You've been vague about the whole thing these past few days, and I'm tired of being put off. I want to know exactly what we're trying to prevent."

"Isn't it enough that we have a plan of attack?"

"No, it's not enough. We're all risking our lives here, the way I see it. And I value both of your lives even more than I value my own. I want to know why we're taking the risk."

Can a person's back express annoyance? Because I think that's what Gillian's is expressing right now. The spatula scrapes along the bottom of the big cast-iron frying pan noisily as she lifts and portions out our breakfasts onto waiting plates. She says, "Sometimes, it's better not to know."

"Come on! I know it's related to Samhain, so what is it?" he asks.

I add, "The zomcopalypse? Opening of the hell mouth?" I probably shouldn't be joking at a time like this, but with Tom so serious when it's usually his job, somebody has to do it.

Gillian sighs, picking up two of the plates and signaling with her head for us to take our places at the small, scarred, wooden table. She sets the plates down and everything just goes out of her at once as she folds limply into her chair.

"I think—I'm not sure, mind you—but I think that Anat plans on pulling the town into the afterlife. Does that answer your question?"

Tom and I must be on the same wavelength, because we both burst out with, "No way!" and exchange a glance before turning back to Gillian.

Tom follows up with, "How could she do that? Living things can't enter the Summerlands." He pauses for a minute. "I mean, can they?"

Gillian leans in, her elbows splayed out on the table top, and her fingers laced together tight. "It's not strictly true that only the dead can enter the afterlife. There are recorded cases in every culture, including our own, in which a living person entered the land of the dead and later returned to the land of the living."

"Like Odysseus?" I ask.

She turns to me and nods. "Exactly like that, sweetheart. If you believe the afterworld is a physical place that beings can inhabit, even if they are only the dead ones, then you have to believe that a living person could visit it under the right circumstances."

"And you believe the Summerlands is like that," Tom said. It was a statement, not a question. Tom knows how fervently Gillian believes in the Summerlands, hoping that her deceased husband Martin is waiting for her there so that they can reenter the living world together when it's their time.

"Yes. But..." She looks like she's going to cry.

"Gilly," Tom prompts. "What's the rest of it?"

"The Summerlands aren't made for the living. If Anat pulls that many living souls into it at one time, the result would be catastrophic. Not just for Giles but for the Summerlands, and for the rest of the world." She stops and sighs, working toward regaining control.

"In what way?" Tom says.

"The Summerlands could cease to exist."

Tom and I exchange another glance. This time one of confusion.

"What do you mean?" he asks.

"Destroyed. That's what I mean. With the scales tipped to unbalance it against the living world, the veil between the worlds could go 'poof'. Gone. Kaput. The veil unveiled. And that will leave nowhere for people to go when they die."

"What?" I ask, my voice going up the scale a little higher than I'm used to. I sound like some stupid, scared little girl. But really, "What?" High, scared voice again.

"There would be nowhere for people to go when they die. The world would be burdened down with the dead."

Tom reaches for my hand and holds it tightly. I don't think he even realizes it.

"What does that mean?"

"I'm not sure, Tom. They get back up and walk around and that zomcopalyse Cassie mentioned happens? They continue on as spectres here after their body decays? I don't know. But the arrangement of the living and the dead as we understand it would be disrupted. It would become something other than it is."

Tom's hand grabs tighter onto mine. "We're going to stop this," he says. "Do either of you even doubt that?"

I try to rally with a smile, but it kind of fizzles.

"Et tu, Cass? Come on! All three of us were there when we put Anat in her place before. Think about it—she's stuck in a smelly, leg-humping, cat litter-eating stray. And who did that to her?"

I guess there's cause to smile. "We did. Well, not me, really. I wasn't myself. But you and Gilly did." I reach my other hand across to Gillian. She perks up a little and takes it. Then she reaches the other out to Tom, who grabs it and squeezes.

"We're unstoppable," he says. "We're unbreakable." He smiles at me. I beam back. "So, let's eat before our food gets cold. We need to keep our strength up for saving the world tonight."

***

We huddle over the map as Gillian points to the critical parts of the pentacle again. "We've got one spot that's still a mystery, but if we've got it right, we know where Zelda, Deborah—or maybe Dash, but let's hope not—and Robert should be stationed. We also have an idea where Anat will be, assuming she'll want to be at the center of the action. That leaves Nat where Cassie was originally placed, since that's the only place without an initial."

As she uses the map for a visual aid, she says, "I think she's going to use them like...well, batteries. Magical batteries, if you want to think of it that way. They'll each need to send their power to the correct location across the star, and once that's completed, it will concentrate in the middle."

Tom puts his hands down flat on the table and drums with his fingertips. "And that's what we need to stop, right?"

"Yes, we need to break those lines of power. I just...Tom, I understand why you want to go for Anat first, but I think we should free Natalie before you do. Her magic will be critical to Anat's plan. Once we've freed her, she can help us free the other witches. Now, Zelda and Deborah, I doubt they're even being controlled. They'd cooperate if they knew it was Eunice they were working for."

"Fine. You and Cassie can do that. But I'm going for Anat. I don't know if I can take her out or not, but if I can, wouldn't that stop it all by itself?"

Gillian's mouth compresses with tension before she says. "I don't know. It's just guesswork, isn't it?"

And it is, it really is. But it's all we've got.

THE COTTON CANDY I'm picking at is the same color as my lip gloss, but it sure tastes a lot better. I go to give my short, blonde wig a tug and remember just in time about my pink fingers and think better of it. There's a definite carnival atmosphere in downtown today. Booths packed with touristy treasures or greasy, sugary carnival foods stand like shanties along each side of the street.

I walked by the "Cinful Readings" booth on my way here, and one of the first things I'm going to do when all of this is over is give Cinnamon a big apology and beg her to do readings in the shop. A third party in my relationship? I should have known it was Anat.

I used to love the Witching Faire when I was a kid. It's like a big party with a supernatural theme. I guess a lot of people in town always knew it was a lot more than that. There's me, always the last one to catch on.

From a distance, I watch Tom as he ducks in between two of the food stands with one of Gillian's big, old suitcases, rigged up with some suspicious-looking wires poking out the top, and we've even thrown one of those big old alarm clocks inside so that it ticks if you put your ear close to it. Tom's idea. He still thinks clocks and bombs should tick. Maybe the cops are old skool enough to expect that, too, but I doubt it. Although in Giles, they definitely might buy the idea of a geriatric bomber.

Tom looks pretty suspicious himself in the tightly pulled-down hoody that hides his who-wouldn't-melt-when-they-saw-it face in the shadows. His ensemble completes with some baggy old jeans we bought at the thrift shop and a pair of old galoshes. That way, if anyone else sees him drop the suitcase, they can back me up with how the guy who left it looked like someone who was up to no good.

He walks by and turns his head to me slightly to give me a wink as he goes. After he disappears into the crowd, I go over to the stand to buy a drink and happen to notice an abandoned suitcase at the side. Imagine that.

"Hey, is this yours?" I ask the kid who waits on me.

"Is what mine?"

"The bag at the side of the stand?"

He lifts up the canvas wall to take a look and says, "Nope."

I ask the kid in the next stand. The response is pretty much the same. Except she says, "A guy came walking out from between the stalls a while ago. Maybe it's his."

"Yeah," I say, "But why would someone leave a bag in there? Seems suspicious to me with all the terrorist activity going on these days. I don't like it."

The kid rolls her eyes and says, "If you're so worried about it, maybe you should report it to the cops. They look bored." She jerks her chin toward the end of the row where one of our local officers is enjoying a giant, greasy-looking elephant ear, then she dumps a big plastic bag full of fries into a wire basket and drops it into a fryer. "I'm sure they'll want to know all about the big terrorist threat at the East Podunk carnival." The sound of the frozen potato hitting the hot grease almost overwhelms the last part of her sentence. But I catch the sarcasm over the sizzle.

I give her my snarkiest like-I-care look and say, "I think I will."

I head for the cop, not one of the ones I know, which is good, because that means he doesn't know me, either. Unless they're all under Anat's control, he shouldn't send up an alarm. I hope. I check my wig and dark glasses are still in place anyway. Just to make sure.

"Um, sir?" I begin.

The cop turns. He doesn't say anything. His breath smells faintly of rum, and his eyes look a little glazed. They focus on mine after a second. It reminds me of how the cops always looked after drinking Kevin's control potion. I try not to cringe.

"There's an abandoned suitcase between the food stands over there," I say, pointing, "and the kid at the stand says some suspicious looking guy dropped it off and then walked away. It doesn't look right to me. Can you take a look?"

He nods and walks over to the suitcase. I follow. Maybe this will do it. If we can get the police to clear the Faire because of a bomb threat, we can get all kinds of innocent people out of the way.

The cop's radio sparks to life. "All units, there's been a code yellow called in. Code yellow."

"What's a code yellow?" I ask.

"Not your business."

But I know what it is. Tom's done the second part of his job and called in the bomb threat.

We get to the food stand, and I say, "See? There. It's got wires sticking out the top."

The cop walks to it. Bends down. Looks at it for a minute, considering the wiring, then nonchalantly unsnaps the latches and opens it up.

I gasp. I have to make it look real, right?

"Yeah, I'd say that's some threat you've uncovered." He dumps the suitcase and the wind-up clock inside it into the trash. "Some kid with a crappy sense of humor," he says. "Or maybe *you* wanted to stir up trouble?"

"What? I was just reporting something that might be dangerous. I mean, if we were at an airport..."

"Aren't you the Granby girl? Eunice Granby's granddaughter?"

"No."

Hells, maybe he does know me.

"I think you are. Mayor Andrews said to keep an eye out for you." He grabs for his radio with one hand and his other hand grabs for my arm.

I don't wait around for it to make contact. I'm running, threading my way through the throng of people like a rat in a maze. Fortunately, I'm better at mazes than the rat behind me, and I'm faster, too. I duck behind a tent and ditch my wig and glasses in the trash bin behind it. I take a garment out of my backpack by feel and then pull it on over my clothes after putting my backpack on backwards so I can reach it from the front if I need to. I pull the long zipper up from my crotch to my neck to cover me and my bag, and then I feel for and pull down the veil attached to the hood and walk back out into the crowd. I've never been invisible before, and I'm not sure I believe it, but I'm careful to dodge the people who can't see me now that I'm dressed in Tom's magic coveralls. I don't need anyone slamming into me.

Not a single set of eyes flicks toward me as I walk by them. The cop who was chasing me is standing by a food stand, his eyes searching the crowd. They pass right over me as I walk by.

The coverall legs are too long for me, and I'm afraid they'll trip me up at just the wrong moment. I stop and hike the suit up around my waist and fold and tuck the extra fabric in, hoping it will keep them snugged against the tips of my shoes so they don't drag.

A random thought about how Tom got the suit floats to the surface of my brain, and the thought of Kreepy Kevin causes an involuntary shudder to move through my body. It's not like Tom will have run the suit through the laundry. Bits of Kevin's skin and boy fluids are probably still lingering around on this thing.

No one would blame me for the shudder.

***

I perch on the pedestal of the statue of Giles Corey, a guy from a town or two over who was pressed to death under a big rock during the Salem witch trials, and who our coven renamed the town for after all that craziness died down. He was apparently something of a local hero. He knew the names of the real witches and didn't give them up.

When I asked about it once, my granny gave me the history and told me the statue was installed in the early sixties, when no one got bent out of shape much anymore about the idea of witches. Or, at least, there hadn't been a mass execution for a while.

Scanning the street from my vantage point, which has a good view straight down the line of stands and attractions when I look to the right, I recognize Zelda at the far end, standing in the spot on the map that was marked with a Z and had the symbol for chaos next to it. She's Gillian's and my second target as soon as she meets me here. It's good to know we got that one right.

I look down to the other end of the street, where the shops that were converted from the old houses start to be replaced with shops and offices built in the fifties and sixties. That's where we expect Natalie to be.

I don't see her, but I do see Gillian where she was going to wait for me near the Decent Food Mart just past where the street is cordoned off. The crowd isn't much of a crowd all the way down there—never really is since sweet Mr and Mrs Rao have never caught on to how their lack of a deep understanding of the English language has derailed their business.

But with the lack of a crowd, that's probably why no one goes to help a pudgy, elderly lady in a flowing hippie dress who's backing away from a huge, snarling, black dog with all the speed a senior citizen can muster.

GIVING CASSIE the invisibility suit was the right thing to do, but I could sure use it about now. There's no sign of Anat's doggie host out on the street, and I'm not eager to go exploring through the shops. She and her enchanted crew could have anything rigged up inside.

Cassie fixed me up a packet with a pair of boxers in case I have to call on Cat and then need to shift back so that I'm not stuck outside totally exposed later on. I always have my hidden caches of clothes around town now, too, where I can grab something and throw it on if I need it.

Cat may not mind letting it all hang out, but things have changed for me since the wallowing-naked-in-the-mud freedoms of Woodstock. My point is, I'd rather be covered unless Cassie's the only other person in my general vicinity. I'd hazard

233

a guess that's what she prefers, too.

I scan the street from right to left, in front of the stands that line the closed street, then duck in back to go along the sidewalks that lead to the shops. In front of the bakery, a kid dressed in black with a pointy cardboard wizard hat and a face painting of a spider grabs his mother's hand and points up toward the top of Cat's Magical Shoppe.

My eyes follow where he points.

It can't be.

Nat is up there on the roof of the shop, standing on the widow's walk. How did she even manage it? There's no door or hatch onto the roof. The flat widow's walk is purely decorative. I've prowled every inch of that big old Victorian in my time. If there'd been a way up there, I'd have done anything to get closer to the birds that roost on its short, white picket fence.

I'd say she's got about the best vantage point to take in the entire Witching Faire. And it would also put her smack-dab in the middle of the downtown pentacle. But Anat's not with her. It's just one of the pups standing next to her, his black fur a contrast to the white slats.

The red purse hung over one arm tells me that Nat's definitely still in there somewhere. Because Nat doesn't go anywhere without that purse. That has to be a positive.

The glowing ball of magic that dances on the fingertips of the arm she raises in the air tells me that her witchcraft is also doing just fine. Not so positive. Her lips move as she addresses the sky. I swear the damn dog is grinning.

Let's see...enchanted witch on the roof of a three story building with no way up, and all I have to do is get there before whatever spell she's spinning is done, break the enchantment, and get her to stop the spell.

No problem.

Piece of cake.

I'm on it.

***

My body twists and jerks and contorts through the shift and Cat lets out a long yowl of pain when he finds his voice at the end of it. The transformation takes longer and hurts more when I'm in a hurry. When Cat's just interested in eating the stinkbug crawling up the wall of the parlor, it happens easily.

Well, not easily, but it doesn't feel like I've been run over by a steamroller. More like I've been run over by a steamroller while under mild sedation. Which—trust me on this—is an improvement.

It won't do to think about it any more, though. Time for this cat to focus.

Climbing the tree is easy, natural. The kind of thing we do all the time. But this time, we're not going in the second story window. We won't be able to access the roof from there. No, we've got to keep going, higher and higher, where the branches thin and bend beneath Cat's weight, threatening to let go.

But we've got this.

The branch flexes sideways and I dig my teeth into it just in time. Cat's back left leg loses its purchase and slips off the branch. Then, the right leg goes as well. The branch bobbles twice but stops its downward motion, and I'm left hanging from a swinging branch by my teeth and front claws, back legs scrabbling inelegantly against the sky.

Cat has to chill out so I can think. It takes every bit of power I have over him, but his back legs stop running through the air.

The only thing we can do from here is ease out farther along the branch and hope for a toehold on the gutters at the top of the roof. Just try to convince a terrified Cat of that. And a terrified cat-shifter. With one life left, I can't afford to splat myself all over the ground and leave my friends to get sucked into the the afterlife before their time.

I hang on with Cat's sharp teeth as I force him to unfurl one set of claws and move it further along the branch toward the shop and grasp the branch firmly again, claws digging into the tender bark and green wood below. Then I remote control him to do it with the other, bringing it close to the side of our mouth. Once I'm sure both claws are dug in as far as they're going to go, I unclench Cat's teeth and let them slide carefully along the branch, ready to clench down again in a second, moving along a fraction of an inch.

At our current rate of speed, we should make it to the roof a few days after Christmas. And I've got a ring to slip on a delicate finger when Christmas hits. I'm not missing that for anything.

I kick up the pace. As the branch gets smaller, it's even more important to make sure I've got a good grip, but not so slow I won't be tucked up in bed with Cassie tonight after I get this tiny glitch in the plan smoothed out.

I'm nearly there. I reach one of cat's feet toward the roof, claws splayed, and it scritches against a metal gutter and catches. Just a little further and I can drop onto the roof...

And then I'm sliding. The branch is too thin now, my claws don't stick as the twigs shred under them. I feel Cat's eyes widen until I'm sure they'll pop right out of his head. It's not gonna make a difference this time that he always lands on his feet. They'll break beneath him. The fall is too far, too many stories below. My back foot goes into the gutter, but the claws there don't have the grasping power of the front ones.

Oh hell, I've lost control of Cat. The feel of his fear burns in our bowels like acid.

His front legs flail out as he grabs first for the branch that's snapping away from him, then at the trough of the gutter as his body passes it.

And he manages it.

Three claws catch, but the pain is intense as he clings to the gutter with the sharp rim biting into his paw. I wrestle control back and pull up to grab onto the wood shake roof with the other set of claws.

We made it. We've got a solid hold. We scramble onto the roof, ready to rumble.

Cat has a short memory for fear. Mine is somewhat longer. I hold him back, now that he'll share control again, while I take a mental deep breath and push away the intrusive image of falling to my death while Giles burns.

THE SQUARE WIDOW'S WALK at the peak of the roof is the only flat space, so I take Cat to the top side of the chimney and have him brace himself there before I whisper my shift words. It's not ideal. It's too soon. The pain will be even more intense than before. It has to go quickly, with no noise, so that Nat and her hell hound don't realize we're sneaking up on them. The noise from the carnival below should cover us, but I keep as tight a control on my vocal cords as possible while they twist themselves from something that can voice only a meow to something that can manage speech.

I feel scraped and raw from the rough brick chimney against my skin, and I'm pretty sure I've got a backside full of splinters from the roofing, but I grab the tightly compressed packet containing my lightest-weight cotton boxer shorts off my collar and scramble into them. I'm not flashing my goodies to the whole town during Witching Faire. No, The modern cat-shifter needs to be prepared.

I could creep up the roof quietly on hands and knees, but I don't need more splinters lodged under my skin today.

What the hell. I stand up and move swiftly toward Natalie, bounding over the foot-high picket fencing easily.

A bare foot catches. I go down fast, landing on my hands and knees. Too bad I didn't think about what I would do once I got here. I'm on my knees five feet from her without a plan.

Natalie turns to my crash landing, her eyes blank at first, then registering anger. She heads for me, hands still raised, the sky-magic forgotten as she comes. I scramble up, backing into the fence, but there's nowhere to go.

She's going to kill me.

She moves a hand away from the silver tendrils in the sky and reaches for me: I duck and weave, dart around her, and rush the pup who's been trying not to get my notice from behind her.

Its jaws open wide and it snaps at me, eyes glowing crimson. I feel the dog's pull on my human mind, and I know Nat's turning behind me. I feel the sizzle of her magic growing stronger on my bare skin, and the urge is telling me to turn, to embrace her. I begin my turn, but Cat's not having it. There is no way a dog can override a cat's instinct.

As he swipes out at our enemy, I come to my senses and remember I have no claws. I grab the beast around the neck and toss it underhand into the air beyond the roof.

It hits the street with a crunching thud and a truncated yelp.

The sound of gasps and startled confusion drift up from below.

"Tom?" I hear behind me. That sounds like Nat. Except a lot less cocky than Nat.

Man, I hope it's Nat, cocky or not. Because if it's not Nat, I'll be following that dog over the railing.

I turn, and her face is a mask of horror.

"Tom. Goddess save us!" She stares up at the silver tendrils swirling above, slowly pulsing outward toward the five points where the other enchanted witches wait. "You don't know what I've done."

"Something to do with the underworld, we figure. You can stop it, right?"

"No, I can't. The spell can't be unspelled. The only way to stop it is to keep it from being turned inward at each of the five points of power. If that happens, if that pentagram completes...." She sucks in a deep breath. "No, we have to stop it. But no matter what, it's already doing damage. There'll be places where the veil will open, but it should close again without any major consequences, without staying open and swallowing us whole if we keep just one point of the star from being turned back to the next.

We have to get to the others—they're placed to deflect the magic just so...." She stops to catch her breath.

I jump in. "The witches make the points of the pentacle, right? That's what we figured out. Gillian and Cassie were going to get you free and then go for...wait a minute—we thought you'd be at the C on the map, where we thought Cassie was supposed to be. Who's there instead?"

"Anat. Anat's there. With Darrin."

My throat constricts. I left my lover and my friend to face Anat alone. And no one even thought about Darrin being part of this. He's a low-key guy, but his calm hides a lot of power. "We need to get off this roof. Now."

Natalie rummages in her purse and pulls out a slim shard of charcoal and a small yellow candle from a silver cigarette case. She draws a circle on the rooftop with the charcoal, then sets the candle in the center and lights it. She speaks some quiet words, picks up the candle, and blows it out.

"Offer me your arm, please," she says, setting the candle aside.

I always do what Nat says, unless she's having a pervy moment. I'm pretty sure even Nat wouldn't decide to have one of those right now. She steadies herself against me as she reaches out to tap the center of the circle firmly with one foot. The piece of roof within the circle falls into the house and lands below with a soft pwuff and then a harder thunk as it bounces onto the hardwood floor.

We're right above a lumpy old feather bed—a favorite sleeping spot for Cat over the years—that's been stored in the attic for as long as I've lived in the shop. I'm sure it's no coincidence Nat picked this spot for her hatch. Each of us sends up another cloud of dust as we hit the mattress below.

As soon as my feet meet the floor, I tear toward the stairs with Natalie behind. She calls after me, "I'll get there as quickly as I can. And Tom...with the veil parting, there might be..."

But I don't hear her last words. All I can think of is Cassie in danger.

***

I'm halfway across town when my brain, and them my body, freezes dead in its tracks. The woman in front of me...it can't be. I say, "Mom?"

She turns to me. And it's her. Wearing the same awful, blue housedress that she wore in the morning every day when she served me bacon and buttery scrambled eggs for breakfast and packed my lunch before she sent me off to school. She looks older than she did then. I bet she never stopped wearing that housedress.

"Tommy?" she says. Her face lights up when she recognizes me. "It is you. Are you..." Her face falls.

"No, not dead? You can't be. You're so young. I've been waiting for you, sweetheart. Why didn't you ever come home?" She moves toward me, and I wrap her in a hug. She feels so alive: her hair still smells of that herbal shampoo she used. The one I bought her in Eunice's shop before…

"I'm not dead. I can't…I love you, Mom," I say, as I tear myself away from her and start toward where Cassie may be in danger. I turn back, unsure, but she's already fading, one hand reaching out to me. I could take it. But I think of Cassie and launch away again, threading my way through the mix of the living in their costumes and what I now recognize as the dead pushing through.

I can't help the dead, can't be distracted by them, but I can still help the living.

"HEY, BITCH!" I yell. This girl can't hide any longer. Tom's invisibility suit is now safely stowed in my backpack and that granny-stealing demon will know it's me. The suit won't work on a dog, anyway. I also may need Gillian's help, and she's going to need to locate me.

I call out to Anat, and her eyes cut to me, away from Gillian. They glow like super-hot iron as she turns her head and snarls. Just behind her, Darrin raises his arms to the sky. Of course the town vet would end up in the pentacle—he'd take in a stray in a heartbeat. Darn it! He's such a nice man. He really helped Cat out when he got hurt last summer.

Darrin's chant is low and insistent. I track his eyes to the sky where the bright silver ball of what can only be magic hangs above the center of the town. Five tendrils reach out from it, waving randomly like an unstuck starfish.

When I look down at the dog again, she has turned back to Gillian. I guess she doesn't think I'm much of a threat.

"Cassie, get out of here," Gillian yells, although her eyes never leave the dog's gaze. She's breathing hard like she's exerting herself in some way that I can't see. Her words are labored, forced. "You know she wants you. You have to get away. I don't know how much longer I can resist her. And once she has my power..."

Something changes then. Her body had been stiff and alert, but now she relaxes, turns to look at the sky where Darrin's eyes had gone before, and she raises her hands toward it. She begins chanting as Darrin falls to the ground. He's not moving, but I hope he's breathing.

I get it: Gillian is a way more powerful witch than Darrin. And I just screwed up her focus so that Anat could get to her. The Anat-dog's eyes flick my direction briefly: she hasn't forgotten I'm here. She's probably thanking me.

I move cautiously behind her, out of range of the freaky red eyes she keeps fixed on Gillian, and hope that she let go of Darrin because she only has the oomph to control one person at a time.

I also hope that poor Darrin, who's been the town vet for like a hundred years now, isn't unwilling to put down a healthy dog, no matter how mentally rabid it's become. Because the thing is, even though I told Tom I could, I just don't know if I can kill her.

After Blackie, what happened to him, even though I know it had to happen that way...my head still flashes me the image of that poor little guy dying. The feeling it gives me is a stain on my heart.

When I get to him, Darrin is moans quietly as he surfaces from the enchantment. I help him sit up, and he orients himself quickly. When he sees Gillian with her fingers shooting out silver sparks now as the tendrils in the sky lengthen to come meet them, and then Anat, teeth bared and spit dripping from one corner of her mouth, he turns to me with a questioning look in his eyes.

I put a finger to my mouth to keep him silent. There's no point in drawing Anat's attention. I'm sure that she's got at least a little surveillance of us going on somehow. There's no point in broadcasting our intentions.

I help Darrin up, and we move away to conceal ourselves behind the corner of a shop. We're both standing with our backs pressed against the side of the building, breathing heavier now that the direct sight line to the enemy has been removed.

"What the Sam Hill has been going on?" he says.

"You were enchanted by one of Anat's minions. Gillian thinks it's so she can yank the town into the afterlife."

His eyes go wide. He opens his mouth but no

words come out.

"It's okay. We've got it handled," I say. I didn't even convince myself with that, but he closes his mouth, and I continue, "We just need to get Gillian back and stop Anat. Any ideas how we can take out a big, goddess-infested dog with really sharp teeth without getting killed in the process?"

"I don't even know how I got here...let's just say I was hoping you already had something in mind."

"The veterinary hospital is pretty close, right? Do you have anything we can inject her with that will put her to sleep for a while? That would do it. Give Tom time to get here and deal with her, at least."

"I do. But how will you get close enough?"

"You wouldn't happen to have a tranquilizer gun? With the darts?"

"No. We don't get that many rampaging lions in Giles."

I roll my eyes. "You just go grab the stuff. You might want to load up a dozen needles or so with the tranquilizer just in case. I'll worry about how we deliver it while you're gone."

"So, any reason why my great aunt Gertrude, whose head was severed by a tractor blade in the fifties, is having a walkabout?"

I look in the direction he's pointing. Yep. Fifties lady. Severed head under her arm. "Dunno. I'd hurry, though."

Darrin rushes off down the sidewalk, eventually getting deeper into the groups of people, some of whom are starting to look overhead or notice the nice lady at the end of the street beckoning to the silvery lightning bolt.

It's only a matter of time before everyone catches on. I feel the pull of the wind toward the magical light show above us, trying to lift me toward it. This is really starting to suck, in more ways than one.

***

Nothing much changes before Darrin gets back. I stay hunkered down behind the wall of shop, keeping an eye on Gillian and the dog as the magic moves through her. If the same thing is already happening at all points of the star, we're already sunk.

It almost startles me when Darrin shoves a small, flat, black leather case toward me. I didn't hear him approach over the increasing roar of the wind. "They're in here. You've got six chances to get the contents of one of those into her bloodstream. The dose is definitely strong enough to take down a dog that size."

I lean in closer so he can hear me. "It won't kill it, though, right? It's not the dog's fault Anat decided to move in."

He shakes his head. "It shouldn't, unless you hit

her with all of them at once. But Cassie…although I'm not completely sure what's going on here, I *am* sure that if Anat's behind it, and you have no choice, you can't worry about sparing that dog's life…"

The image of Blackie with a pencil sticking out of his eye socket hits me again. I push it away. I sure won't be effective in a fight with that picture stuck on the internal slideshow.

"Yeah, I know." I take a deep breath. "Here goes nothin'."

I walk out on the street and head straight for the goddess who tried to steal my body and my boyfriend last summer and nearly succeeded. Here's hoping I can think and react as fast as my heart can race, because with what's going on inside my chest, I'd out-think and out-react her before she knew what hit her.

*****

I go around the back of the building and enter the alley, then I travel through the narrow grassy area between the shops and exit close to where our friendly neighborhood bitch goddess has Gillian under her nefarious control. I creep forward as quietly as I can. I can't tip her off that she's under attack. I picture myself as a cat, moving as soundlessly as Tom would on soft, padded feet.

It's working. I'm ten feet behind her now. I've

got the first needle out and ready to plunge. I thought I'd get as close as possible and then do that repelling thing, but she hasn't turned yet, and getting right up next to her and stabbing it in would work so much better. My aim will be pretty good when I'm standing right next to her, at least.

I creep forward a few more steps.

A few more.

I'm almost close enough to touch her. I clutch the first hypodermic in my hand.

Gillian turns, her expression a big blob of nothing, one hand still to the sky, the magic streaming into it now. The other falls limply to point right at me.

The dog, which I thought was paying me no attention at all, doesn't even glance my way but coughs out a woofing laugh I know is meant for me. I turn and run for it.

It's no good running. I'm being pulled down the street. Slowly, but insistently. I turn and lean back against the pull, trying to back myself away with my feet planted firmly one step at a time. But the soles of my sneakers don't have enough grip to fight this force. I slide slowly toward the rift.

A tendril the color of the magic in the sky winds around my waist. Go-juice spikes into my bloodstream as I dig in and push, but it just gets tighter around my middle, taking me slowly backward in its grasp.

I claw at it, but my hands just go through. I

can't tear it off. I throw myself on the ground, landing on my hoody pocket full of syringes. I hear the crunch as the glass smashes and the precious serum they release soaks into my clothes. I try to dig my fingers into the asphalt street, but there's nothing to get a hold on. I scrape along the ground painfully, slowly, but without any ability to stop myself.

I lift myself up as far as I can, find Darrin running toward me and shout to him, "Go get Tom. He's at the magic shop."

Then I turn toward Gillian and push my palms outward with some magic action of my own. Repelling again. This time for a reverse tractor beam effect. I may be a one-trick pony, but it slows my movement down, at least.

I hope Tom doesn't take too long. Because if he does, I'm going to be the first one among the living to pass through the veil to the underworld.

"TOM!" DARRIN CHARGES toward me, out of breath. I keep up my own pace as I approach him. This can't be good.

When he reaches me, he bends over, putting his hands on his knees, trying to catch his breath. He gasps, "It's got Cassie. And Gillian. We tried to knock it out, but..."

"Where?" I demand. He points to the northern edge of downtown, where one of the tendrils of magic glows stronger than the rest. It looks like it's almost at its target. There isn't much time. And in this crowd of living and some dead now solidly blocking the way down the street past the gazebo, I need to be small and swift.

I don't care who sees.

I duck into an alley and before I'm fully hidden,

I shift. I run out the back of it in a blaze of feline fury.

***

I blast toward the action, catching glimpses as I duck around the legs that get in my way. There's a rift in front of Cassie, and she's being dragged down the street toward it by an invisible force. She has her feet clamped against the pavement, sitting and leaning back, but she's still moving forward, inch by inch. Another world, sunnier than I would have thought, shows through in the spot where the veil is torn, a few curious dead lining up on the other side, some of them daring to cross over.

Cassie tries to stand but her feet are pulled out from under her again as she slides slowly toward rip in reality.

Why are the living just standing around? Why aren't they screaming and running? In fact, when I glance over my shoulder to look back down the street, it looks like the crowd has gotten denser since I came though it. Yes. It is. People are coming from the center of town, gathering to watch.

They must think it's all part of the show! They're still killing time until the drawing at the gazebo. I'm sure no one wants to have their name drawn, not be present to claim it, and have it pass to someone else.

Still, maybe it's better for everyone if they think

it's a play put on by the council. Panic isn't going to help. But I sure would like more of them to be on their way back out of town, just in case Anat finally has her way with all of us.

Looks like some of the witches are catching on. There's a little exodus happening at the back of the crowd now. It's subtle. They're backing off, but they're keeping an eye on it. Maybe some of them will help if we need it. They see Gillian as an ally, so why should they think she's a danger now?

Gillian's eyes fix on the thickening strand of magic in the sky, but when it reaches her outstretched hand, she drops the hand toward Cassie and skewers her with a thin stream of magic, accelerating her forward movement. Cassie resists— her own palms glow as she holds them up against the force. But she can't beat Gillian and Natalie's magic combined, she isn't strong enough. And she may even be holding back because she doesn't want to hurt a friend.

From behind it all, the inky black bitch with the bright red eyes gives new meaning to the expression "never trust a smiling dog." Anat can smile all she wants, but her plan for this town isn't going to happen. Not with me and Cat on the scene.

I've cleared the last of the onlookers now, and with a new burst of speed, I blast around the filmy rift and leap onto the dog's back, getting my sharp, sharp teeth into one floppy, smelly canine ear. She tries to shake me off, but I keep my grip, anchoring myself with claws dug in tight. I can distract her, but once I do, it's up to Gillian and Cassie to free themselves.

The dog yelps when I rake across its sensitive nose with one angry paw that swipes out from my stranglehold around its head and neck. I hope it's Anat who feels the pain.

It snaps and growls and shakes its head, but its teeth never reach me as I hang tough, swinging loose and falling to the side, but regaining my grip at the nape of her neck, teeth still dug in, giving me a firm hold. I pull my head back and grip the dog's ear even tighter, sending the animal into another frenzy of yelps as my teeth come through its soft flesh on the other side.

I could shift now and ring its neck with my strong man hands, but I'm not sure I could keep my grip through the transformation. I'd be vulnerable if it didn't work. Cassie would be vulnerable. I can't risk it.

Cat isn't strong enough to do much damage. I'm going to have to hope that my efforts are loosening Anat's grip on Cass and Gillian. Or that Nat gets here to help. ecause the wind keeps building around me, rushing toward the hole between the worlds. It isn't long before all of us are going to have to find an anchor and hunker down or be pulled in.

***

"Anat!" a female voice cuts above the rush of the wind. "You lopsided, feral, old canker! Come pick on someone who can put up a decent fight. Kittens and puppies? Dear, dear me."

Man, am I glad to hear that voice. The dog's yelping and shaking is scrambling my brain. Just once I'd like to hear Nat cut loose with a bona-fide cuss word, because when she does it's going to be a doozy. But for now, lopsided canker will do.

The dog's head snaps to where Nat's voice came from. I wobble as she turns, but when her head stops, I see Nat in front of us, just to the side of the rift, blindfolded but giving every evidence that she can see just fine as she strides toward us.

"I'll bet those eyes of yours are a bloody red right about now, trying to dig into mine, aren't they?"

A deep growl sounds from the throat my front legs are wrapped around. Anat's attention is fully on Nat now.

I drop off and hit the ground running toward Gillian, who's dropped the hand she held pointed at Cassie. Her chubby face is a mask of alarm. The rift Cassie was sliding toward vanishes. Cassie stands up and backs quickly away. She puts her hands to her mouth and her eyes fill with tears, but I can't go to her and comfort her yet.

Darrin has, though, and is pulling her back away from whatever specter upset her. She might still be in danger—I need to get her out of here—

but Gillian has no one to help her.

Gillian stands still, breathing deeply. As I rush to her, I see the cogs turning for her again now that Anat has let go. But a huge ball of magic is building up on the hand she's no longer pointing at Cassie. That stream has to go somewhere. She's supposed to turn it, to make the point of the star. And that's the one thing she cannot do. If she does, the small rifts happening all over town will join into one big dance party of the dead.

That magic has to go somewhere harmless.

Up in the sky, the tips of four other streams have been caught and deflected back. They travel again toward the center, picking up speed. If Anat turns her attention back to controlling Gillian, or any other witch in the vicinity, we're all going to hell.

Not me. No, I'm not going anywhere. Not when I have so much to live for. After one last glance at Cassie, I rush to Gilly and rub against her legs to get her attention. If my idea works, it'll probably make a mess, but it won't destroy the town. I can't waste precious time shifting so I can tell her directly. I have to make her understand me before that big ball of danger she's burdened with decides to make its own move.

I start digging at the ground like I'm burying something untidy. This is one that we're not going to want to see again. I lift my eyes to hers—no, she's not getting it.

I dig furiously at the asphalt with my paws again and lift my eyes to hers one more time. She smiles.

"Move! She shouts.

I don't hang around to find out what happens when she buries it: this mess is gonna need a big hole.

From a safe distance, I turn, and the stream of magic is disappearing into the ground, blasting through the asphalt, the edges burning like lava. As it does, the power behind it begins to drain away. The stream thins, dims—all of the streams do—as the lines that cross above downtown begin to slowly snuff out. Relief washes over me.

I look down the street to the small rifts that dotted the way, and the dead are beginning to fade. I recognize one of them just before he goes, his eyes locked on Gillian, his face infused with joy. I wonder if I should tell her that if she'd turned just in that moment, she would have seen Martin, too.

WITH GILLIAN SAFE, I rush to join Nat in her battle against the cause of all of this. My former enslaver, the goddess Anat, proof positive that the gods must be crazy. Once I stop her, Cassie's finally out of danger.

Nat's standing her ground, still blindfolded, her hands held out in front on her, moving as Anat moves, tracking her. They fizz with a blue charge that isn't electricity. I think she's using magic to "see" what's around her in a way that doesn't put her at the risk of whatever bad juju Anat pumps out with those neon eyes of hers.

I take my place at her side, ready to dart in if she needs me. Somehow, she knows I'm there. "Stay put, Tom. I have a plan, but that doesn't mean it won't go south."

I twitch my tail and yowl in response. Best I can

do under the circumstances.

Nat reaches a hand out to where Gillian is stuffing the last of the magic stream into what is now a wide hole in the street. She motions the magic toward her, nonchalantly, and it leaps from Gillian's control to her own. "Now let's just see who'll send who to the underworld," she says to her slobbering enemy.

She doesn't get a chance to start another taunt. The dog leaps, horrifically fast. Natalie doesn't react. Maybe she doesn't see it. Maybe Anat can block the magic Natalie is using to sense what's around her.

Cat never thinks of consequences. Our body crouches, springs, and flies up into the dog's face, all claws and vengeance. A distraction. To give Natalie time to complete what she began when she took back control of the spell she started on the Magical Shoppe roof.

How many times is Anat going to snap Cat's neck before he learns?

The answer to that question comes to me on a wave of regret, as it all fades to black: twice. She's only going to snap his neck twice. This time, we've run out our full nine lives.

"DARRIN, I'M FINE. My hands hurt, but it's no biggie. I need to help with Anat."

"Cassie..." he says to me, shaking his head, but probably already knowing he's lost. He's not keeping me in the shelter of this alley when my friends need me. "Let me just finish dressing this before you go out and get more." He bandages the scrape he'd just gently cleaned asphalt dust out of and opens his hands in a gesture of submission. "Go on..."

I dash back toward where I last saw Gillian and Anat. Natalie's there now, and the lines of magic in the sky are dissipating. The last strand rushes toward her waiting hand and she compresses it into a ball in the other. It's difficult moving toward them—people are starting to realize now that something isn't right. They're hustling down the street away from the scene, a sound of raising voices rising over the street, building into a murmuring wave of confusion. I have to duck and weave as I make my way against the tide.

I don't know what Natalie's planning, but I'm pretty sure Anat isn't going to like it. I don't want to see some innocent, possessed dog wiped out when all it probably really wanted in life was a warm place to sleep, regular meals, and a stick to fetch. But the raging animal it has been turned into isn't going to be pacified with a rawhide chew toy.

I take in the scene. Cat is at Nat's side. Nat is blindfolded, but definitely in command of all her faculties. A silver thread of magic curls in her hand as she pulls it from the sky. Gillian is peering down into a big hole in the street, looking weak and used up. I start to detour toward her so she can bring me up to speed and maybe tell me how I can best help, but before I do, the Anat-dog takes a giant leap at Natalie. It's like it can fly—it almost covers the fifteen feet between them until a much smaller black ball of fur flies up to meet it.

It all happens so fast.

The dog's front feet hit the ground, still a few feet from Natalie. A small black body flies from it's mouth when it shakes its head and flings it away like it's nothing.

My scream drowns out the sound of Natalie opening a rift around the dog with the magic she called down from the sky. The dog slides backward toward the underworld, taking Anat along into the land of the dead, where dead things like her belong.

Too late to save Cat.

Too late to save Tom.

Natalie gets to him before I do, and she tries to grab me, to keep me from seeing, but she's still dealing with Anat with one hand while she reaches for me, one hand toward the rift, the wind tearing at us, roaring around us. I push her aside and get down on my knees next to his limp body. His neck lies at an impossible angle from his body, red trailing from one ear to wet his sleek, black fur. "He said nine lives. Nine lives. That's all Anat gave him." As the sobs shake me, I raise my head to Natalie, screaming, "Why didn't you stop him?"

"It happened too fast. I didn't know what he was going to do."

"Shut up, shut up, shut up. I don't care. He's gone. Anat finally got what she wanted. She destroyed everything that was good in this town!"

Gillian appears at my side, reaching out to me, but I push her away. I can barely breathe. I gasp for air, curled over Cat's small body. Why does she think she can comfort me? I turn to them, hysterical, sobbing, "He's got to come back, he's got to! It's just taking longer is all. It's just different somehow from the other times..."

Gillian shakes her head, tears welling up in her eyes. "Cassie, I think...I'm sorry...I think he really did only have nine lives." She reaches out for me again, but I slap her hands away. She looks stunned.

I turn to her, screaming, "Fix him! What good is all your magic if you can't fix him!"

She doesn't have an answer. She just backs away. And then her eyes are drawn behind me, and they open wide.

She whispers, "Cass?"

I turn back to Cat.

And it's weird. Like beyond weird. My sobs stop dead. There's a guy growing out of Cat's shell, tiny at first, pushing his way out of Cat's mouth, the skull breaking and fur stretching thin, tearing apart, dropping off in bloody red globs. It's obviously Tom's head pushing its way out as he gets bigger, and then his shoulders appear, then all the rest of him, full-size. And all I can really think is—no matter how relieved and full of joy I am—I never want to see anything so freaky again.

I laugh hysterically with tears still streaming down my cheeks while Tom becomes Tom again.

When it's done, the cat-skin lies on the ground, stretched, shredded, nothing cat-like left. I throw myself at him and cover Tom's body with mine, getting sticky in the goop that sticks to his skin, which is probably Cat's insides. But I can't be sad for Cat right now. I smother his bloody mouth with kisses.

When he opens his eyes, he asks, "Is this Giles or the Summerlands?"

"It's Giles. Anat lied. It was only Cat who had

nine lives."

He smiles, looking tired but otherwise unaffected, his brown eyes fixed on mine. "When I saw you, I assumed it had to be heaven."

"I think you might get a break and land there with clothes on if this was heaven." I smile and dig through my backpack. I pull out a pair of shorts. He pulls them on quickly and I pull him close to me. He shivers. His sexy flannel boxers aren't going to keep him warm in this weather.

Our reunion is cut short when Nat shouts behind us. Tom bolts up, unsteady. We turn as one to the sound. Gillian and Nat are sliding along the street in a repeat of my own performance, their shouts for help blowing away as they scrape along the asphalt, picking up speed, toward the rift that gets larger and larger as the black mist of Anat's soul leaves the dog and her magic pulls them toward her. She's the one holding the rift open now. She must have latched onto Natalie's magic somehow and turned it to her own use.

Tom streaks toward them and grabs Gilly by one hand and Nat by the other, then pulls back, but he can barely hold them. He fights the pull as he walks sideways toward a lamp post, the women's feet still pointing toward the hole in the world as he goes. He helps them get a grip on it and they cling there. I run to join them, fighting the same pull, my hair blocking my eyes, leaning left to stay upright.

When I get there, all of us hang on to the cold metal post against the force coming from down the street. Natalie pulls her blindfold off and it flies down the street into the widening crack in the universe.

"My purse, Tom, my purse," Natalie shouts above the sucking sound of the wind, "Open and aim it toward her. Don't let go of it or close it until every speck of her is inside and my chant is done."

Tom slides the purse down Nat's arm and she lets go of the pole briefly with that hand as Tom snatches the purse away.

"Hold it open, Tom. Both hands. It will close if you don't." His eyes cut to mine.

"No. Don't let go," I plead.

Natalie's voice cuts through the roar of the wind again. "Do you think this pole will hold against her? Do it, or we'll all go together when it's uprooted and pulled in."

As if to illustrate her point, one of the lamp posts in front of us crashes to the ground and flings up showers of sparks as it scrapes along the ground in a rush, disappearing into the chasm at the end of the street.

Tom uncrooks his other arm from around the pole and turns to face the dark smoke that's arranged itself into the form of the goddess. She looms in front of the hole into the underworld, smiling. Tom leans further and further back against the gale force that's pulling at him, nearly sitting now, his feet still sliding. He maneuvers Nat's purse so that the mouth faces Anat when he opens it. Makeup and potions and a flapping pair of black cotton gloves fly out into the mouth of the underworld and are gone.

Natalie begins chanting. It's nothing I understand. And it's so quiet. How can it possibly save us?

And then...

The wind eases—not stopping, being itself sucked toward the opening of Nat's purse when an opposite force pulls back at it. Tom lands on his butt hard when the pull stops and the smoke-demon Anat is stretched into a streaming funnel of black rushing toward the open maw of the purse.

With a whoosh, it sucks her in. The gale stops when the last wisp of smoke disappears into the bright red purse and the threat is gone. Nat's chant goes silent.

Tom snaps the purse shut, then turns back to us, handbag hanging from one arm now. He's grinning a lot more broadly than most men would who've been left minding a purse.

The rift closes as though it had never been, although Giles looks like it's just weathered the worst nor'easter in history.

Nat, Gillian, and I let go of the pole, our hair and clothes in disarray but still stuck to living bodies. We exchange relieved looks as Nat bitches,

"I'm really going to miss that purse."

Yep. Everything back to normal.

***

"Might as well enjoy the rest of the Faire," Nat says, smoothing her hair back into a tidy bob and straightening her clothing. "And there's still the small matter of a mansion to be raffled. I certainly don't want to miss that. Though, with its history, I can't imagine why anyone would want it."

The rest of the three of us give her looks, then Tom shrugs, hands her the purse, and takes my arm. We wait for him while Tom puts on the rest of the clothes from my backpack because wandering around in plaid flannel undies isn't the best idea in late October. Darrin joins us. Nods are exchanged. We're all still a little shell-shocked.

Then, we walk back toward the center of town, where people are starting to congregate around the gazebo now, still buzzing about the entertainment they just witnessed. Some of them point at us. Others wave and shout, "Great show!"

The witches give us knowing nods.

Robert scans the crowd from the gazebo as we approach. His face brightens when his eyes alight on Gillian. He rushes down the steps and comes toward us, his eyes never leaving hers through the crowd.

When he finally lets loose of her long enough to speak, he says, "Something happened here, didn't it? But for the life of me, I can't remember what it was. I was at the edge of downtown with only the haziest memory of how I got there. And then everyone's telling me what a great show the town put on this year."

Gillian rubs his back gently with one hand from where she is still snugged firmly into his side by his left arm. "Long story. I'll tell you when you've got a drink in your hand. I think you'll need it. For now, you have a mansion to raffle off." She looks at her watch. "Yes, in just about ten minutes, according to the Faire schedule."

He raises his eyebrows at that but doesn't say another word.

***

"He really is terribly dashing, don't you think?" Gillian whispers to me as Robert addresses the town from the podium set up in the Gazebo.

I nod. He is.

But Tom's better.

I squeeze his hand where he stands at my other side, his full attention on Robert's speech.

Robert is talking about the drawing now. The old Stanford mansion is really quite a prize—it's supposed to be pretty much a time capsule of the town. When old Hetty Stanford passed away—she was nearly a hundred—she left the mansion and its contents to the city.

But some people say that's just because no one in the know would want it. It's supposed to be haunted by the spirit of Giles's only mass murderer, William Stanford, who disappeared after killing five of his neighbors. Most people stopped visiting Hetty long before she started actively keeping people away. Sightings of William's ghost were frequent.

Robert stops talking—it was all just blat, blat, blat to me anyway because all I can really think about after our close calls is keeping a tight grip on Tom's hand.

I sneak another look at him: his attention is still focused on the Gazebo as Robert reaches into an old straw hat to pull out the winning raffle ticket. Robert looks surprised as he reads, then smiles.

He looks up and announces, "Well, this is very fine. Very fine indeed. It's nice to see the Standford mansion end up with the heir of one of the older Giles families, recently returned to take over his family's old business." He dangles a set of keys in front of the mic as he leans in to say, "Tom Sanders, would you please come pick up the keys to your new home?"

I turn to Tom, and he's beaming. I ask, "When? What? You put your name in the raffle?"

"Hey, a guy's got to plan just in case the world doesn't end. I never told you how I feel about it, but I don't think I can keep living forever in the place where I was enslaved. I have so many happy memories there now, but...."

Wow, am I a failure as a girlfriend or what? He shouldn't have had to tell me it was difficult for him to stay at the shop: I should have known. Sometimes I'm just so stupid.

I ask, "You think there'll be room there for one slightly dense but very loving girlfriend? Because I sure wouldn't want to keep living at the shop without you."

He kisses me on the top of the head as he pulls me toward him. "I think that can be arranged." He grabs my hand and turns toward where Robert still waits, looking expectantly in our direction.

"Let's go get the deed to our new home."

He rushes along so fast I'm afraid I'll fall, but if I do go splat, I'll still be smiling.

I HOLD CASSIE'S hand while Robert lets go of Gillian's long enough to step into the side mirror view of the cement truck and direct it to back up until the long chute is placed directly over the hole that had been dug for Anat's prison in Corey Woods. Magic can forge a pretty good prison, but a few tons of concrete will last longer.

Robert holds his hand up for the truck to stop and then walks to the driver's door to have a quiet conversations before the gritty gray cement starts to flow. Then he walks back to where Cassie, Gillian, Nat, and I stand to watch as the hole slowly fills. Robert connects back with Gillian, grasping her hand tightly. Only Nat is singular, clinging to the handle of the flashy red vinyl purse that saved us all.

When the hole is half full, Nat hands me the purse, "You do the honors, Tom. None of us would

275

be here without you."

Her expression when she lets go is sad, scared even, for just a moment. That's not like Nat. I don't know what that's about. She'd taken the purse back and held it for safe-keeping since the day of the Faire, carrying it with her everywhere for the past two days. I don't know what would make her so reluctant to give it up now when we can make sure it never gets opened.

"Don't want to say goodbye to your old enemy for good this time? I'm sure you can find other ways to keep life interesting."

She glares at me. "I say she's finally where she belongs. But I'm going to miss the bag."

I put my arm around her shoulders, supportive. "Let's do it together." She resists, but then she sighs and lets me pull her in. We stand united as we each find a handhold on the red vinyl handle and swing the purse outward, tossing it into the rapidly filling hole, where it lands with a soft, wet plop. Its red gleam is buried in gravel, sand, and cement within minutes.

"Thank you, Tom," she whispers, too low for the others to hear over the grinding whine of the truck's mixer spinning. "It's more than a purse, you see. It's a ward. One that cost me dearly to create. That's why I knew it could hold Anat. It was designed to keep the spirits of the dead from coming too near. And the interior? It would prevent one from ever getting out. Even a dead goddess."

"Why would you have something like that?"

"Because my family's magic is tied to the other side. We see the spirits who linger instead of passing beyond the veil. We see them all the time..." She takes a deep breath as the truck stops spilling cement into the hole, and she starts to walk away down the path we'd cleared through the woods, no longer facing me when she says, "Can you imagine what that would be like? What was it like for you, Tom, when you saw your mother there in the middle of downtown?"

I grab her hand and make her turn back to me. "How did you know about that?"

"Does it matter?" Her eyes narrow like she's angry, then they widen and she asks more gently, "Imagine if she was there all the time, within your reach, and yet you couldn't touch her."

"I think that would be terrible."

"Yes, Tom. Terrible is exactly what it is."

I give her one more squeeze before I step back to stand with Cassie to watch the hole fill.

When it's done, I walk with my friends back out of the woods, away from the final resting place of the demon goddess who wanted to destroy us all.

The swath of cleared ground that had been made to allow the construction trucks through the woods looks like a wound against the green forest lands. But even now, saplings that were bent but did not break begin to reach upward again, in hope, toward the late fall sun, and our feet stir up a dance of golden leaves as we walk.

Wounds heal. My friends have taught me that.

***

"That's gorgeous. Am I really supposed to eat it?" Cassie says, as I set the pie in front of her. I'd decorated the crust lovingly with raised and cut-out leaves and vines and finished it with an egg-white wash to make it shine with a perfect light-caramel sheen. "And anyway, isn't it wrong to have dessert first?"

I grin. "It's the main course. A meat pie. In fact, I got the recipe from Gillian's stash of her mother's old recipes. It's a little old fashioned, but I've had my heart set on it for a long time. And I'm not going to have any time to cook for you soon with all the work I'll be doing up at the Stanford place to turn it into the Sander's place so we can move into it by Christmas."

"Christmas? That soon?"

"My gift to you. Is it big enough?"

She laughs. "They say size doesn't matter." She grins, her eyes shining me my answer. She loves it.

Then she says, "You know, that pie smells amazing." Her eyes drift back to it. She's getting a mansion, and all she can think about is chow time. She asks, "So, this pie...what's in it?"

"It's pigeon."

"Tom! You didn't!"

She goes tearing out of the dining room, and I follow her out the front door into the street. The setting sun reflects off the line of shop windows in pale reds and oranges. As she exits, the startled pigeon takes off, then circles back to land again on the bench after it realizes she's no threat.

She turns back to look at me. "You are the worst..."

"That's not what you said last night." I pull her into the doorway, where we snuggle tight. "I just thought, in memory of Cat...well, it's symbolism, right? It didn't have to be our pigeon. I don't have the urge to hunt it now that Cat is gone. But everything I've ever hoped for is coming true now, and I wanted Cat to be here, too, in some small way. And there's another thing..." I drop to my knees and pull the small velvet box containing the all-important ring out of my pocket. My heart races as I look up at her. "Will you..."

There's not even a moment when she hesitates.

"Hells, yes!" She laughs, dropping to her knees in front of me so that we're on the same level. "Oh yes, yes, yes!"

My hands are shaking as I try to put the ring on her finger. Hers are, too. It's a miracle we don't drop it and watch it roll into the sewer. Our miracle.

She leans in to me and we smother each other's mouths with kisses, then she grabs one of my hands and pulls me up and along, back into the shop, laughing, floating, crazy with love for her, and then I remember: there's one more thing I need to ask. For Cat.

I stop her just before she lifts her foot to travel up the stairs where our bed awaits. I pull her tight against me and place my mouth near her ear to whisper it.

She leans back and twists to look at me, confused at first, frightened maybe, then intrigued. She smiles, and she says, "Yes."

As a little girl, I wanted the gown, the prince, and the fairy tale. But as Robert wraps a fine cord around my wrist to bind it to Tom's, I realize the only thing I ever really wanted was Tom's hand fasted to mine here in Corey Woods with all of our friends watching. All of them—the witches and the warlocks, of course, but also the ones who have no magic, my friend Daria among them. Even my Dad is here.

Of course, not everyone's invited to the second ceremony, the secret ceremony. I'm still a little scared about it, but I trust Tom. Perfectly.

I don't even mind how cold it's gotten or that a snowflake or two drifts down from a gray sky that promises more. It's Christmas, after all. I know most of the witches aren't into it, but it's still a special day for me.

"Tom, Cassie, this ribbon symbolizes your life together, your love for each other, and the connection you have found that tied you together long before the one here that symbolizes it. But the true ties are created by your pledge to each other, by your vows today, by your two souls, bound now together as one."

I can't take my eyes off Tom's face. I'd pinch myself to see if I'm really awake, but I don't want to wake up if I'm not. I can't believe we're really here together after everything we've been through. I'm sure whatever words Robert said and I repeated were deep and meaningful, but the minute I say them, I can't remember them. Nothing sticks except for joy.

Best. Christmas. Ever.

"Now, to seal your bond. Tom, will you kiss Cassie?"

Tom's face splits in a broad smile. He leans in to our kiss, gentle, loving, and yet fierce. Then we reluctantly pull apart and turn to face Robert, our hands still wrapped together.

"In all things, you are joined." He unwraps our hands without undoing the tie and hands the cord to both of us. Tom grabs me and pulls me toward the cabin we've decked out for the reception where a roaring fire and our feast await.

The snow comes down in soft white feathers now. Everyone loves a white Christmas.

***

With the fire and the mulled wine and the friendship and the scent of the pine, it's the best wedding reception ever. I think we may all be a little drunk when the small group of us gather on the porch, shivering.

Aurelie walks out, supporting High Priestess Maryse on her arm, both of the women wrapped up in huge, warm, and very fake furs. I mean, they're French. Of course they're going to slog around in the woods in style, right? It's just fantastic that they're here. It means a lot to Tom.

We don't have far to walk to reach the ritual grounds. It's stopped snowing now, and the moon is visible, ringed with clouds, but bright and nearly full. We wait as Robert and Darrin catch up, each of them carrying a small travel cage. They set them down gently next to where Tom and I stand, grinning goofily at each other. We enjoyed every minute as we waited for the moon to rise and be our witness for the final ceremony tonight.

Aurelie assists Maryse as she draws a circle around us, making things sacred, making things safe, blessing us before we begin. The others ring the ritual grounds with candles: black, brown, and white.

When Robert, Gillian, Natalie, Darrin, and Aurelie encircle us, just outside the ring of candles, I'm not cold anymore. Not when I'm warmed by the love of the people around me. Tom puts his arm around my waist to pull me close, and I snuggle into him. "Thank you," he whispers, barely audible. "Thank you for being willing to share every aspect of my life.

Perfect trust. Tonight, I need perfect trust in Tom, in my friends, in the Goddess. And it's easy. It's easy to trust every single one of them.

Maryse begins. I don't understand the French, but I don't need to. She motions toward the cages, and I bend to the one to my left as Tom bends to the one at his right.

When we're standing facing forward again, Tom holds a black cat against his shoulder, and I hold Sheba, a long-haired calico, against mine. She's usually queenly, even a little mean, but tonight, under the moon, her heart is racing and her back claws push against me like she plans to run.

Maryse lays one calming hand on Sheba's head and another on Tom's Kit. Both cats relax. They must recognize the high priestess as a friend. She talks to them, soothing.

She's asking permission of them before she begins. Then she moves her hand to Tom's shoulder. He nods. His answer is yes.

She moves to me, and I nod the same. For Tom. To share his life, the full range of his life, I would do anything. And I will honor my animal in all ways.

Maryse nods and motions for us to sit.

It's cold on the inch of snow. It melts into the

seat of my jeans and panties, but I won't be wearing them much longer, anyway.

She lays a hand on top of each of our heads and begins the chant. I feel it first where Sheba lays against me, the urge to combine with her, her body pressing into mine. Mine into hers.

And the pain begins. Tom said it would. I ride through it, trying not to panic, reaching for Sheba with my mind to soothe her, too. How strange it must be for her.

The screaming is horrible from the inside. I can't imagine what it's like out there. Everything contorts: my hearing, my vision, the horrible screaming. Gillian moves toward me, concern on her face, but I'm frightened by her swift movement.

I back away on my black and orange, white-tipped feet. The screaming becomes yowling and then subsides. I arch my back and hiss.

Kit slips up beside me, soothing, his sleek fur sliding against mine. Sheba grasps him around the neck with my neat paws and gives him a playful nip before I get control of her and let him go. We touch noses. Saying hi as the pain recedes. Kit's head, Tom's head—it's confusing—gives me another quick butt to point me in the other direction. I turn, and Maryse and Aurelie have handed their clothes to Robert and Gillian, who fold them neatly over their arms.

The French women move a few feet apart as the others back away to give them room to shift, their feminine bodies going strange until it's finally done.

Where Aurelie had been, now there is the wolf. She'd told us not to fear it. I meet its eyes and I'm reassured. There is something more than wolf shining there.

Next to her, the biggest owl I've ever seen blinks its eyes, then leaps into the sky, winging its way above us for long minutes before it comes back to perch on the wolf's back.

The wolf's big head motions toward the woods, the direction of the musky smells that make my haunches tingle with anticipation of the hunt. We pad along behind our guides to the wild, where we will fully become one with our sacred animals. Me and Tom, side by side. In this thing together.

Epilogue

"You might as well come out. I've felt you skulking around at the edge of every shadow since I had to give up my ward," Natalie says with faked aplomb. The stress rides up her spine in sharp prickles. She's not prepared for this even though she knew it was inevitable from the minute she sacrificed her trusty red handbag for the good of Giles.

And there he is, fading in to nearly opaque. He hasn't changed one bit. He's still wearing that gawd-awful diamond-patterned sweater vest and tie over a tight white button-down shirt and a pair of cotton dress pants. His hair is still cropped short on the side and his curls are brylcreemed into an oily-looking pile on top. A change of wardrobe and hairstyle certainly couldn't hurt. He looks like a child to her now, when she used to think he was so grown up and exciting.

His smile forms from mist. "You're as beautiful as the day we met," he says.

"And you can still lay it on with a trowel."

"You're spikier than I remember, though."

Natalie snorts. "You've been away a long time. Things change."

"You made me go. I didn't choose it. I told you I'd wait."

She turns back to her book, her body stiff. "I never thought I'd need the family magic again, especially this late in life. I'd turned my back on it so long ago that I'd almost forgotten what I am. The dark potential of the magic that lives in me. Where's that blasted incantation?"

"You know it wasn't me who did those things all those years ago," he says. "You've no reason to be afraid of me."

She doesn't look up. "That again? I don't know anything of the sort. Didn't we have this conversation just fifty years ago? I'm bored of it now."

She feels his presence close behind her. She's afraid to move, afraid his essence will brush against her, and she'll be forced to see something from inside it. That's the worst part—brushing up against the pain that lives inside all of the lingering dead.

"Great galloping goblins! Back off," she shouts. "Never get that close to me." The strong sense of him moves away. At least he still pays attention to what she tells him. He was always good for that.

Always polite and attentive.

"You didn't mind when we were young."

"You weren't dead when we were young." She turns and he's back across the room, a safe distance away, hands in his pockets.

His voice is even, but his look is pleading. "You have a point. I can see where that might put a damper on the relationship. But I'm still here. Still waiting for you. You're precious to me, so live a long life. I want you to. I'll be here, still waiting, so we can cross to the Summerlands together."

"Fine. But go wait somewhere else."

"For a while," he says, nodding. "To give you time to adjust." Then he's gone without further ado. A wisp that is no longer a wisp. She casts her senses out for him, but he isn't near now.

She knows she'll have to let someone in on her secret eventually. But who can she trust enough to help her with building a new ward? Her family's taint still hangs over this town every time the old ritual grounds are mentioned. Nobody wants to think about that kind of magic. Oh no, not that. Magic should be clean and sparkly. Doesn't matter that a person can't help what they're born with.

And a fresh corpse to charge a new ward? Difficult to lay one's hands on, but not impossible. It may, she mused, prove more difficult to find a suitable, sturdy handbag in fire engine red.

ABOUT THE AUTHOR

Jill Nojack is a writer, musician and artist. The Bad Toms Series is her second published series.

When she isn't exploring her creative side, Jill enjoys laughing too loud and long in public, long bike rides, and talking about herself in third person. She resides in the great American Midwest with a long-suffering cat and makes her living as a computer tech, because, if you're lucky, that's what you do with degrees in English and Sociology.

You can visit www.jillnojack.com for more info about the series along with Jill's other books. You can also sign up for the email newsletter if you would like to be notified when new books in this and her other series are released.